EXILED FLAME

BY

JULIAN M. MILES

Printed via the Kindle Development Program.
Available from Amazon stores worldwide, and other retail outlets.

The eBook is available for Kindle from Amazon stores worldwide, for Apple devices from iTunes, and for all other devices from Smashwords.

British Library Cataloguing in Publication Data. A catalogue record for this book is available from the British Library.

Design and layout by Julian M. Miles
Original front cover art by Simon J. Mitchener.
Photo of Julian M. Miles by Maricel Dragan.

Visit us online
Julian M. Miles (a.k.a. Jae): www.lizardsofthehost.co.uk
Lizards of the Host Publishing: www.lothp.co.uk
Simon J. Mitchener: www.deviantart.com/simonjm

TOH

"Nineteen, eighteen, seventeen, -"

Liddy's eyes go wide: "She's early!"

Thaj. The last thing we need is something to attract even more attention.

"Scrap the count! Two, one, strike!"

We go through the double doors. Pashta drops the security guards and staff with one shot. Coffee and documents go everywhere as the misaligned suppressor field affects the surroundings in ways it shouldn't.

"What the bloody hell?"

Tarme puts a shoulder into the big man's chest before he can say anything else, then follows him down and chops him unconscious.

Liddy and Kon somersault down the stairs, arriving at the bottom faster than those down there expect. I hear twin impacts. There are two bodies stretched out on the floor by the time we go by, one a guard, the other dressed like the big man upstairs.

Kon kicks the doors open. Tarme charges through, knocking one attendant down and away. Pashta tackles the other off a prone form who is kicking and cursing in Nethalyn.

"*Shon ko,* mistress. Look into that mind. You know these words. We come to help."

The struggling stops. Hazel eyes narrow. Without a word, she gathers herself into a crouch. Tarme catches my eye, waves a finger by his temple in the sign for 'Weaver'. I look back. He's right. Her eyes are leaving tiny trails of sparks as she moves her head. *Thaj, thaj, thaj.* I was hoping for a simple night.

"*Irik'taa,* mistress. What were you?"

The head stops moving and the eyes focus on me. They flash amber, then she looks puzzled. I think we've had dark trouble delivered to us.

"We are Shonnu, soldier. What powerless wilderness have we been condemned to?" She scrapes at her tongue with glittering nails. "What is this language?"

Liddy squeaks. Kon goes white.

Pashta whispers: "*Guthane.*"

We found out last time there isn't a word here that translates that accurately. Which is still right, and still frightening. But I can't let us stall until we adjust. It took a while, last time.

"*Upya!* Let's get gone like we're not limited, people. Double clear."

I help newbodied Shonnu up and beat a hasty retreat. Pashta and Tarme take point and tail. Liddy and Kon pause to arm and release a pair of clean-up drones apiece before following. I hate to waste two, but we can't risk leaving even a slight trace. Not after this.

ONE

The steps are spotless. The two constables at the top are wearing respirators. Detective Constable Pete Reeves knows what happened before the smell of bleach hits him. Getting closer, he can see the pale runnels cut through the grime on the pavement where the caustic mixture trickled from steps to gutter.

He looks up to see Detective Sergeant Meredith Tanner heading his way from inside, complexion showing pale round the mask she's pressing to her face.

Exiting the building in a hurry, she swerves round him and comes to a stop at the kerb. Pulling the mask away, she takes several deep breaths before coughing for long enough to attract the attention of everyone within hearing range.

Pete rests his backside against a rear panel of the patrol car where she's leaning on the bonnet.

"Morning, boss. Something new or a variant of same?"

Meredith raises a finger, takes a slow breath, then hacks and spits into the gutter.

"Both."

She folds and crumples the cheap mask before dropping it in the bin liner hanging off the side door of the CSI van. Grabbing a pair of respirators off a rack in the same van, she tosses one to Pete and heads back inside, donning hers as she goes.

"Come and see."

He hurries to follow his boss down the corridors of New Monument Hospital, one of the first built after the SARS-3 panic of '23. It's bright in here. They tried for cheerful, hit garish instead. It's also very clean. Wide, airy corridors with carpet tiles in beige and cream - where the bleaching drones didn't hit.

The reception area looks like someone was searching for something. Everything has been thrown about. He peers over the counter, then up. Warped tiles floor and ceiling, again. But the coffee stains all over the place are something new.

"Pete."

She sounds raspy. Even with a respirator on, the acrid smell of enhanced bleach warring with neutraliser is irritating his throat. He knows Meredith's got something like asthma: this place must be difficult for her.

"I'm fine. Stupidly thought I could tough it out until the extractors cleared the basement. Had to grab a throwaway mask so I could make it up and out without keeling over."

It's like she heard his thought. Which is why they work so well together – most of the time.

"Must be something new for them to use even more of their mutant bleach."

"This time they were helping someone out."

She pauses at the top of the stairs with the sign saying 'Mortuary Only' on a wall nearby. He stops and points to the sign.

"They stole a diener?"

"What?"

"One of the staff."

She shakes her head.

"No. According to testimony from both attendants, and confirmed by CCTV recordings, they left with one of the bodies, but not in their usual way. Which is why I interrupted your holiday. I badly need your eyes. You've been chasing down the details. I hope you can shed some sane on the crazy we've got here."

He half-bows and swings a magnanimous gesture towards the stairs.

"I'll do my best. Lead on."

Downstairs, the fumes have nearly cleared. It's deserted except for two crime scene technicians, a harried-looking constable, and an irate man in a white lab coat, who lunges toward Meredith as soon as he spots her.

"Did you have to run off? I was about to explain how sometimes diagnosis of death is inaccurate, which this was obviously a case of. Really, there's no need for a fuss."

Meredith stops dead and glares at him.

"Doctor Stansen, the deceased had her head stove in with a hammer, an attack witnessed by three people. That hammer is secured in the evidence room at my police station, along with the testimony of those three people, a paramedic, and two police officers."

"A deep scalp wound…"

She raises her hand: "We'll be in touch," with a nod to the constable, "show the doctor upstairs, please."

Pete watches them disappear up the stairs before letting the incredulity flood out.

"A hammer? Tallia Kinch got up and walked out?"

Meredith shakes her head.

"Identification error. It was Musette Kinch all along. Tallia is flying back into the country to identify the body. A body that apparently came back to life and left the building, ably assisted by our favourite five."

She raises a hand, fingers spread.

"I better get someone senior ready to do the apologising in case we don't retrieve her body."

Pete chuckles.

"Optimistic of you. Getting one back would be our first win against this bunch."

"Just checking my phrasing for the request. 'Ever hopeful' is a popular outlook up the line."

"I'll take your word on that. So, what did the main event look like?"

Meredith points at a wall and whistles. The nearest crime scene technician looks over and waves for her to carry on. She leans on the wall and gestures for Pete to do likewise.

"It was a quiet evening turning into a slow night at the New Monument. The security operator at the desk had been chatting up the new nurse when the mentoring nurse returned from her rounds. There was some banter and the guards by the door stepped across to join in. Seems that coffee was obtained and a relaxed end of day was on the cards.

"Then our five near-invisible assailants came through the doors. Before any of the guards could react, the closest of our raiders took them all out with one shot."

Pete raises a hand: "Using their 'bendy floor' energy weapon, I presume, judging by the aftermath. How many casualties?"

She sighs: "All five. Burst eardrums all round, the operator got a ruptured eye, and the young nurse was partially decompressed."

"She must have been near the centre of the area of effect."

"CCTV shows she was."

"Wish we could get a line on their technology."

"Would help. Shall I continue?"

"Please."

"They stormed on, beat down a cleaner at the top of the stairs, took out the last guard and the other cleaner at the bottom of the stairs. They then entered the mortuary, poleaxed one attendant and smacked the other one into a corner so hard it dislocated his shoulder. But they failed to knock him out. He played dead."

"Smart chap."

"Very. That's how he got to overhear the conversation they had with the former corpse he'd just inadvertently let out of one of the drawers. They escaped as usual: fast, on foot, turned into an alley, never came back out."

"Former corpse?"

"She was staggering along with them. Had something over her eyes that flashed orange. One of the technicians reckons it could have been some eyeware set up to go off every time she blinks?"

"To what ends?"

Meredith shrugs.

"They're stealing bodies from mortuaries and you're worried about their taste in nightclub accessories?"

"No, I'm curious about the change in pattern. The worry is constant. Anyway, I presume the bleaching drones did their usual 'spray everything then spontaneously combust on the roof' repertoire?"

"From the scorched remains up top, they used four. You'd be right: no ignition of anything combustible nearby, but each was burnt to a crisp."

"Two more than usual. Did the attendant tell us anything useful or is he suffering from being bleached?"

"We got lucky this time. None of those sprayed were face up or had prior breathing issues. They'll be blonder and peeling for a while, but the doctors are optimistic about them making full recoveries – from the bleaching, at least."

"So what did the attendant say?"

"That, you need to hear for yourself. Now, take a look about this scene, ask for anything I might have forgotten, then we can head back to the station. The attendant should have been patched up and delivered there by now."

Πυ

"This fane is unfit, soldier."

I look about the place. A converted rooftop space, big enough to be subdivided into individual cubicles, along with a training area, lounging area, and kitchen. We have a bathroom across the corridor, and a balcony with a fire escape at the other end of the corridor.

"This fane is all we can hold and remain unseen, mistress."

Her eyes flash amber again. I brace myself. Her temper gets worse every time her mighty powers fail to do anything except briefly turn her eyeballs into lanterns.

Liddy storms past me and slaps my Guthane so hard it knocks her clean over the side of the armchair and onto the floor.

"His name is Narbyl, mistress, and you better rise from spoilt child to someone useful right quick, or he will see me add another killing to the blood tally on this fane."

She goes for Liddy, screaming rage and more. Liddy knocks her down. What we were does not match what we are. It takes time and effort to adapt.

I notice Kon has placed himself to intercept me should I try to intervene. Tarme likewise.

Liddy knocks her down again.

I lean back and sip my *lakso*. This could take a while, so I might as well steal the moment to enjoy some of Pashta's own blend. It took her so long to find the equivalent ingredients here. I swallow and smile; she's certainly captured the flavour.

An hour later, my Guthane is still swearing like a Guthane really shouldn't while Liddy drags her towards the bathroom by both ankles. Pashta is walking nearby, a pile of toiletries in her arms.

"Now, mistress, we'll take a little break and teach you how to maintain your new form."

The reply is in Nethalyn dockside cant. The act suggested is so extreme even Tarme raises his eyebrows.

Pashta shakes her head.

"I never thought the rumours of your lowly origin to be true. The fact you ably use cant, and know of that act, tells me I was wrong."

The door closes behind the three of them, cutting off the lurid reply.

The silence stretches, punctuated by shouts and screams from the bathroom.

I look toward Kon. He shakes his head. Tarme rests a hand on my shoulder.

"Nobody should meet their Guthanes, brother. Especially not one as loyal as you, and even more so when this one is so brutally fallen."

Kon nods: "Gatchimak recanted before us all, Narbyl. We thought him a pretender amongst them. Now it seems he might have been the honest one."

He's got the right of it. I lean forward until the nausea fades, then look up at them.

"What's he doing now?"

"Carpentry in a place called Chichester. He's reconciled with the family of his flesh, too. Some disease of the mind they have here covers all of it, apparently. When last we talked, it sounded like that newbody Liddy thought would harmonise with him has become some sort of surrogate daughter."

I should be able to remember her name… No. It's gone.

"Who was that?"

"Tershyp."

"Good, good. He needed something to remake himself around."

"It worked. She pushed him to find a stables to slake his thirst for riding. The owner is a good woman with children and no man of note. Gatchimak came across as right content with his new mortal life, even more so with the prospect of being partnered and with family."

If only. I have dreams of being that content.

My other thoughts I speak: "After Heklary ascended, Gatchimak and Shonnu adopted her followers. From that bloody day forth, they led separate, contesting denominations. For all the contradictions and infighting, they were part of the last Trey, and they led *our* lands. With her arrival, we have no fane on Nethaly. We are truly exiles."

Tarme crouches by me: "Ever a truth, for all that you always hoped beyond reason that there was a way back to the Trey you serve so well in two bodies."

Kon kneels before me: "Your drive saved so many. You alone. Not Guthanes, *packan* or *shemsil*. You. It's why we stay. You are the Guthane we owe our second breath to. I beg you, Narbyl, lead us now to find a new way for our new lives. The lands that surrounded our fanes can no longer be anything we would wish to return to."

I've followed self-declared Guthanes, thinking them manifestations of the Unseen That is All. No more.

"You're wrong about one thing."

They both look at me.

"I'm no Guthane. What power I have is what I've trained to be. From now on, we have no truck with any who claim themselves to be manifestations of the Unseen."

The door slams open. Liddy stands there naked, dripping wet, her tan gone whiter than fresh fallen snow. She raises a shaking hand.

"Long ago, every Guthane agreed to each raise two of their most deserving attendants to assist with the rigours of overseeing the paired worlds. Those mortal incarnates were unaware of the limits implicit in their creation. They plotted long, eventually turning on their creators. Most failed. The few successful ones were executed by the remaining Guthanes. All except our two, because our Guthane actually deserted them."

I turn my gaze away so I can think: I didn't know two of each Trey had been created by the third. Nor was I aware their oversight included both Nethaly and Kethany. What we were told was incomplete, and the rumours weren't quite accurate. But, she's not saga telling, she's shocked to the core. Which means -

"What new truths have you about our two?"

"Heklary didn't abandon us. Shonnu exiled her whole!"

I'm standing, legs shaking. I don't remember getting up.

She who smiled so tenderly as she touched my infant brow, banishing the water fever and freeing me of disease from that day forth, could still be manifest, somewhere.

Kon rushes to Liddy. She hugs him, whispers something, then takes her lithe form back to the bathroom with an unsteady gait. He walks slowly back to me. I feel myself age a little as he approaches.

"She's here. Whatever residue of Heklary survived the expulsion ritual, is here. Just like all the rest. Just like us."

There's a loud 'splash' from the bathroom.

My legs give way.

Pashta comes in, drying her hands. She looks me straight in the eye.

"That treacherous incarnate is dead."

My rage gutters and dies. In its place is resolve.

"A new start we shall have. But first, we must reckon and forecast. Shonnu arriving explains the lack of predictions after her. Whatever transpires on Nethaly, or on Kethany, they are likely done with complicated ways of getting rid of the inconvenient. While waiting long enough to confirm that, we have our Guthane to find, or her death to confirm, or a search until we reckon a decent enough attempt has been made. Then we will find a place to found a new fane for what will be our second new start."

Tarme looks to Kon: "What is this Chichester like?"

Kon smiles: "From what Gatchimak tells me, it seems goodly. But who wants to bear the news?"

Playing the messenger to one renowned for epic rages. Arriving to tell him that his downfall was likely by the hand, or at least the betrayal, of the one he regarded as blood kin? If I were them, I'd want better armour. I myself might be able to get away with it. But, I'm in no hurry to test that.

Pashta looks at each of us.

"Leave it until the time comes?"

We all nod.

TWO

Druid's Hill is an old police station, but it's weathered the years well. One of the longer-serving staff told Pete it used to have a medical centre where the workshop is, and the screened cells he's sitting in one of used to be part of a single shielded room. He looks about. Place must have been huge.

Meredith comes in with a well-built young man. His clothing is in complementary shades of red, except for the thin black sling supporting his left arm.

"Pete, this is Oswald Achebe. Oswald, this is Detective Constable Peter Reeves. I'd like you to tell him what you told me."

Oswald sits and takes a moment to settle his injured arm.

"I was on duty 'til midnight. Denny had just come in. He'd swapped part shift with Reina so he could go to the match yesterday afternoon."

Meredith types a feed from her phone to the terminal in front of Pete:

> > Denny Carmichael, mortuary attendant, was knocked out, suffering a grade three concussion in the process.
> > Reina Sambor, senior mortuary technician, no noted criminal activity.

> Hospital records show the half-shift exchange between them
was properly booked and approved.

> The 'match' was Chelsea Amazons vs. Detroit Dark Angels.
(Amazons lost 19-31.)

"He'd just gowned up when we heard this freaky noise. Sounded like bones breaking. We hunted for it and Drawer Sixteen was where it was coming from. Denny stepped back. I reached for the drawer handle. It all went quiet inside. I opened it and there's this orange flash, then the body comes at me. I'm not ashamed to say I screamed. Who wouldn't? So, she's not dead and she's not making sense. I'm trying to get her off me, calling for Denny to help me hold her until she calms down, but he's just shaking his head and backing toward the doors.

"Then I've got my hands full, too busy to look about. There's this 'crash'. I hear Denny yell, then someone pitches in and tosses me into the corner. I'm a hundred and ten kilos, mister. Got swatted off like I was some mongrel. I hit the corner and felt my shoulder give like something lit it on fire. I decided lying still and pretending I'm out cold was the best way to deal. I stopped moving, bit down hard, and shut the hell up.

"First thing I heard ain't like no language I've ever come across. Then some bloke says they've come to help. Said something about understanding. Then he asked the damndest thing: asked what she was. Not who, but *what*. The reply was odder. Really thick accent. Said she was 'Shonoo'. Called him a 'soldier'. Then she raved a bit before he gave orders and everybody left.

"I stayed put until some sort of acid cloud rolled in. So I grabbed a mask from the cleaning rack and ducked into the shower cubicle."

Another update comes up on the terminal.

> Which is where he was found. Battered, shocked, and very wet.

Pete leans forward: "What did she rave about?"

"For real?"

"Might be relevant. Tell me what you remember."

"Sounded like two badly pronounced questions to me. Think she asked *where* they'd been condemned – she definitely said 'condemned'. Then asked what language they were speaking?"

"The orders?"

"Pretty sure it started with a swear word, I didn't understand it. Then sounded like 'get gone liqueer nut lim tid'. His accent had thickened up. Like my uncle does when he's stressin'. But, the last thing the soldier said was 'double clear'. I'm sure of that."

Pete nods.

"Thank you, Mister Achebe. We'll find someone to run you home."

Oswald shakes his head: "Can you get someone to take me to wherever Denny is instead? He's got nobody to watch over him."

Pete glances at Meredith. She nods.

"We can do that."

He sees she's already routed a request to the front desk. They wait until a constable comes to collect Oswald, then he swaps to Oswald's seat while she takes the console seat. She pushes his display from terminal to his phone, then pushes her display from phone to terminal.

"Thoughts?"

Pete stares at his interlaced fingers.

"'Double clear'. Doubling the number of drones used? Seems to match up."

"Give you that. Anything else?"

"They're not locals. The odd language. Poor pronunciation. Maybe some fallout from another civil war England profited off before leaving both sides high and dry? That thing about orders works for me, too. I'll take that as confirmation they're military or ex-military of some kind. Meaning their modus operandi is backed by planning and experience. It also suggests to me the cadavers they take are not targets of opportunity. They come for a chosen body in each case."

"You thinking North African Alliance?"

"I'm thinking from somewhere in the mess referred to as the Nordic Independent States. Those zones never really recovered from the Three-Day War, no matter what the media would have us believe."

"True. Want to turn this over to Counter-Terror, then?"

"Why? I'll give you that their technology is worrying, but it's nothing anyone has, and I've checked thoroughly with our military liaisons. If it was something attributable, they'd have had this off us like a shot. Either they're letting us do the boring bit so they can swoop in at the end to take the credit and the tech, or this is something they're not interested in.

"Right now - excluding today's living dead girl - all we have for certain are thirty confirmed breaches of the Cadaver Disposition Act by a small group of persons unknown. Some, or all, of the thefts may also fall foul of the Anatomy Act 1961 and/or the Human Tissues Act 1984."

She raises her hand: "I read that section of your detailed report. It can't have become any more interesting, so skip it."

"Always the critic. Don't know why I put up with you. I could have got a paying gig by now."

"You love it, Reeves. Get on with you."

"Slavedriver." He grins, then points to the notes they have on their screens. "Okay: I see no real terrorism angle. None of the deceased died with or from anything on the HCID list, nor were they carrying biological hazards of any nature when they passed. The other seventy-two body disappearance cases I have tentatively linked to ours fall under various 'lost due to acts of weather, disaster, or shoddy filing' clauses."

"Except Henrietta Lawson."

"Hettie is a unique case, I'll give you. Died five times on the way to the hospital. Pronounced dead the sixth time she went while they were operating, only to revive a few hours later in the morgue. Eventually found wandering in a nearby park, complaining of a headache because someone called 'Lanta' kept shouting at her inside her head. She's currently under observation at King's College Hospital. Apparently, her Beta waves are abnormal, the voice in her head is now screaming, and she spends a lot of time under sedation."

"I still think you should go and interview both of her."

"You're not funny."

"I know. Don't care. What next?"

"Wait for Musette's body to turn up."

"Now who's not being funny?"

He laughs.

"What's not funny is me spending the rest of the day reviewing video of the streets around the New Monument Hospital in case one of the cameras caught a glimpse of our elusive body snatchers."

"You go and savour that. I'll go request the necessary reinforcements to greet and pacify Tallia Kinch."

"Armed Response?"

She grins.

"More like someone who can pass for beautiful people. You know the type: good skin, nice breath, lots of rank badges, a smooth manner, and an expense account bigger than our departmental budget."

"Good idea, boss. See you later."

TAΠ

"Never thought I'd be so happy to see one of ours disappear into a rubbish bin."

Pashta grins.

I choke on my *lakso*.

"You did what?"

"Slung the useless *crepsty* headfirst into a bin. Don't look at me like that. I picked a yellow one. She was definitely a 'Biohazardous Waste'."

I wave my hands, splashing *lakso* about, until Tarme grabs my arm and de-mugs me.

"Yellow, now? That has to be somewhere that is watched."

"I had my wrap on. They got nothing. There's only a couple of constructs watching that cul-de-sac. Think one of them is dead, anyway."

I slam both fists into my thighs. The pain overrides my mute attack.

"River! I said no sewers and drop her in the big one after dark! It's mid-afternoon! You *drowned* her in our bath. They may be confused, but you keep making it obvious and they'll be on us right quick."

Liddy leaps in my lap, evil grin on her face.

"Weren't you the one who taught me about not accusing until after I had gathered all the facts?"

I catch my breath with difficulty because she keeps poking me in the ribs at half inhale. Finally, I manage to bat her hand away.

"What did I miss?"

She jack-knifes off my thighs and lands on her feet.

"Me sticking a suppressor wand down her throat and popping her breathing sacks. She came up from the water gasping, arms out gripping the sides of the bath, mouth wide open. Too easy. I used the lowest setting. Sure, she expanded when it hit, but nothing tore. She went all floppy, though."

'Bloodthirsty'. That's how Kon described Liddy. I keep forgetting I have to consciously commit details to my faulty memory. The forever recall we were born with was a function of our previous bodies, not the essence they sent here. Did they really care if we died? I often ponder that. What possible reason bar cruelty could they-

"Narbyl!"

That's the other problem. Effortlessly being able to do things while getting other things done, sometimes with links to *lathny* weavers too, is no longer possible, for all that my mind keeps trying. Here, I have difficulty remembering, and have to do all but the simplest things one at a time or I lose focus: chasing a thought instead of paying attention.

"Sorry. Linkthought."

Liddy dodges my feeble block and taps my nose: "Muddlethink, that's what Tarme calls it."

I look at Tarme. He spreads his hands, fingers on both making the sign for 'don't shoot me'. Kon sniggers. I'm outgunned and these incorrigible newbodies have the right of me... Again.

"You might be right, but don't expect me to like it anytime soon. So, Shonnu is a sack of butcher's offal. You bleached her?"

Liddy looks smug: "Even dowsed her original deathblow and did something like it. Then I bleached her."

I wave at Kon.

"She really enjoys it, doesn't she?"

Kon smiles tenderly at Liddy: "She kills like we breathe. 'Enjoy' is the wrong word."

Liddy puts her hands on her hips and sticks her tongue out at him: "Wrong. I enjoy killing for some people."

She winks at me as she turns away. That is meant to tell me something. Or tell me off. Not sure. I miss things too often, and things like that I've never been good at.

Pashta shakes her head and waves them away.

"Go and roll in each other's fire for a while. Tarme, war counsel us."

Liddy and Kon sprint toward the bathroom. Tarme wanders back from the kitchen with fresh drinks for the three of us.

"By your leave, Narbyl."

I duck my head: "Please, skip the formalities. We're a long way from the high steppes."

Pashta sips her tea and sighs.

"Long may that remain true. Never have I been so cold."

"Icy Tursht deserved his reputation, I'll admit. But forcing even his own people to use *lathny* to maintain their hearth fires? I always thought that harsh."

She purses her lips.

"He didn't. Tursht got the secret of *esseny* from Haglin. Those fires burned from the essence of prisoners."

Using that which enlivens our bodies as fuel? All of a sudden, I'm a bit more enamoured of remaining here. Enough. To the planning.

"What of our conduit supply?" I sigh: "Remind me what they call it here again."

Pashta beats Tarme to it.

"Copper. It is plentiful here. I can find us scraps in every edifice. Were we to need quantities, it would be easy, but getting larger amounts would certainly attract attention, some of it sure to be of the wrong kind."

Tarme nods to her.

"Truth spoken. They have so much here, it is dizzying. I can hear it sing all about us as the sun traverses the sky, even hear it hum under the full moon. So much, and some of it so pure, it is almost criminal to lower it to weaving."

Finally I understand.

"Though we're reduced, it is the purity of the copper in this world that allows you to replicate the weavings?"

"Truth spoken. Without the purity, we'd be bereft."

He gestures to the workbench in the far corner.

"With Pashta's gifting, I have woven us all suppressor wands, realigned all the guns, and fortified our wrappings."

"Pashta gifted what?"

"Two nights ago I procured us a far better batch than any we've had before."

She gestures as if referring to some trivial effort. I know it wasn't.

Tarme stretches, a satisfied expression on his face.

"From now on, they might catch glimpses of us with their constructs, but what is discernible will certainly be useless."

I shake my head.

"I still feel that standing out here is undesirable. We must strive to use woven devices last. Even though they have not yet grasped the principles, they will be eager to seize our weapons. We must consider them as capable as any renegade weaver hold."

Tarme shakes his head.

"Our constructs are useless without the ability to use *lathny*, which hardly any of them possess."

I look at him, my disbelief writ large on my face. He smiles.

"We can all use it. Few of us are strong enough to weave, even in small ways. Like you, for most it is only revealed by our ability to use *lathny* constructs. For others, it also shows in ways like Liddy's essence perception."

I sit up, spreading my hands while making signs for 'caution' with my fingers.

"Truth spoken. But, I still think it best we be undetected, rather than unidentifiable."

They nod, slapping left hand to right shoulder as they do so, the salute due a *shemsil.*

"Enough of that, too."

They grin.

"So, give me your counsel on Shonnu. Do not spare any depths in consideration for my bruised loyalties, either."

Tarme runs a hand through his thinning hair.

"That she has been sent is a final act. We know many of those delivered here since Gatchimak were opposed to her. It seems to me her attempt to become a true Guthane failed and she was served as she had dealt. The sort of thing that loyalists of Thurgil would consider fitting."

They certainly would, and him having been the closest Guthane to our lands, it makes sense.

"So you believe our lands are now Thurgil's?"

Pashta leans forward: "Who would gainsay it? A true Guthane stepping in to end her rule and enfolding her benighted denomination whole, cleansing it of her in the same way she'd disposed of others: a fitting rite of adoption. The news we got from those we saved certainly gave the impression of her becoming more and more tyrannical."

I'd taken the news we got as nothing but the extreme views of exiled fanatics. I now believe my dedication to the ideal I held of the Trey has been more fanatical than all their efforts put together.

"I have to concede you're both likely right. Details are irrelevant, Liddy can feel no approaching essences out to the furthest extent of her reach, and that has never happened before, neither here nor there."

Tarme sits up.

"She felt essences arriving on Nethaly?"

"That, and those passing toward Kethany, too. Once or twice a year."

He raises both eyebrows: "Interesting. I'll need to think on that."

"Is it relevant?"

He shakes his head: "No. But it's enlightening. Some of the more obscure writings I learned may become clearer with that knowledge."

Pashta groans.

"More being kept awake by your pencils scratching on paper early in the morning."

"Then give me evenings twice a week."

She laughs.

"Cunning of you. I agree. But only if the days can change from week to week."

"Acceptable."

He chuckles.

I head for the kitchen. They'll be wrangling over duration next, then on to rearranging their training sets to allow him the two evenings free. Who am I fooling? I might as well sleep. It'll be dawn before they're done. I glance toward the bathroom. No. It's sleep or wait. One of the oldest training tips I got was 'always sleep when you can'. Choice made, then.

THREE

Pete looks up as a constable rushes into the detectives' section and enters Meredith's tiny box of an office without pausing to knock.

He's out of his chair and reaching for his jacket by the time she comes out. Spotting him, she waves for him to join her and heads for the rear exit.

As he catches up, she flashes a smile over her shoulder.

"Guess whose body just got found in a biohazard skip down the road from here?"

"You have *got* to be joking."

She stops, turns to face him while wiping her security pass on her sleeve.

"That's exactly what I said to Officer Budesman."

She slides the card through the elderly reader. It considers for nearly ten seconds before flashing green and releasing the door.

"As crime scene scanning and analysis have finished, they're moving her back to the mortuary she was taken from, with the addition of a quartet of AFOs to toughen up the security."

"Four armed officers? That will certainly stop any enthusiasts. Not convinced our quintet will be so easily deterred if they're of a mind to."

"I know. I tried explaining but got overruled. Apparently you're a good detective but prone to seeing threats or even conspiracies where none exist."

"One case. Eight years ago. Still think I was right, and I'm sure it got handled off the books."

"If it's any consolation, they did mention something about ignoring national security concerns being bad for your career."

"Not funny."

"Not joking."

Pete stops and looks at her. He can't make out her expression because she's partially silhouetted against the afternoon light at the top of the vehicle bay exit ramp.

He decides to take the comment at face value.

"Well I'll be damned. I was right and they'll never let me near anything with a whiff of secrecy ever again. But it does prove this body hunt is a minor case."

She shakes her head.

"I thought you'd go ballistic. That'll teach me."

"What's the point? Fighting the system is a privilege reserved for those without their lifestyle depending on it, or the fanatical few of those with little to lose."

"A remarkably cynical and resigned viewpoint, especially coming from you."

He steps closer and gestures for them to walk and talk.

"That case I fell foul of involved a friend. Two years after, unrelated in any way, my half-brother spotted something odd at Ashford Freight Terminus. He rang me to get an idea of the investigative processes that would occur – he gave me several scenarios, didn't specify which one was the one he'd stumbled on. Said he'd come round after reporting it and tell me the whole story. That night he died in a traffic accident on the way home. Next day my place was searched while I was at work. They removed their presence from every camera feed except for a discreet unit I had outside my place. If I hadn't had that, I'd never have known."

"What did you do?"

"Erased the external recording. Relocated the unit. Some matters are best left undisturbed."

Meredith nods.

"You definitely reached 'no fool' the hard way."

Pete nods.

She points toward one of the newer-model electric saloons.

"Going up in the world, boss?"

"Mine's in for an overhaul. Got this one for a week to help the techs get some real-time evaluations on the new software."

"What about your late-night kebab runs?"

"Part of the deal is daily diagnostics downtime between 23:00 and midnight."

"Nice. Do I get to dr-"

"No. Why do you think mine is in for overhaul again?"

"Dad was a rally driver. He taught me as soon as I could reach the pedals."

"So you keep saying. When I asked your father about it at the last Christmas do, he said he stopped teaching you because you're a 'fucking lunatic when you're behind the wheel' – and that's a quote."

She points: "Passenger side. Go."

"Spoilsport."

"Precisely. This isn't sport, this is urban driving."

"I could have been a contender."

She grins as she turns the saloon towards the exit.

"For some things, you still are."

"Low blow, ref."

"Shut up and register us rolling out in a new unmarked vehicle. They haven't hooked these into the duty boards yet."

"Will do, boss."

RHÍ

"Narbyl, my *packan*."

That whispering voice is familiar.

"Wh'zit?"

She makes a startled noise, then coughs loudly.

"Liddy. Remember me? Titchy, fast, dangerous? Pashta said you need to get up because we might have a problem."

I sit up.

"Problem? Approaching essences?"

"No. One just popped up."

"Where?"

"At the hospital we last raided."

Now what on this world, or our two, could that-

Hold that instant.

"Pashta! Didn't Shonnu sojourn with Haglin?"

There's a moment's muttering, then she shouts back.

"Tarme reckons that rumours of her time on Kethany could be true."

"Could she have learned *esseny* while she was there?"

Tarme steps into view.

"Given her fire aspect and love of shedding blood for the slightest reason, it wouldn't have taken her long, either."

She'd been powerless, then killed. Dead for the final time. But, that one tiny chance?

"Wrap up! We're going up against prepared forces this time. Dress with care and bring everything. Kon, you're carrying the drones. Liddy, you're our *klemdonar*."

They all stop moving.

"Yes, we're going to be pack-wise, and have her ready to come down like magma rain - when the trap closes, or they think they have bested us."

FOUR

Doctor Stansen peers down at the head of the body on the table.

"Reina, come and look. It's just as I suspected: the head trauma isn't as severe as initially reported. I knew they were wrong. All that fuss. What a mess."

The cadaver opens its eyes. Amber flames fountain from the empty sockets into his face.

Stansen makes a mewling noise. Reina turns. The doctor's head is shrouded in silent flames. As she opens her mouth to scream, he falls onto the body. The flames whirl toward her. Reina screams.

The armed officers outside react almost immediately, drawing pistols as they turn to the doors.

Entering the mortuary, they see a body in a lab coat sprawled across a corpse on the table. The other figure in a lab coat is reeling about at the far end of the room, head completely obscured by what looks like fire. As the doors close behind them, the flames seem to go out.

They advance. The figure, now discernible as the female mortuary technician, brandishes a surgical saw and advances on the pair. Her face is contorted with effort, her movements jerky.

"Miss! Stop moving!"

"Put the weapon down."

She snarls and lunges. The officer on the left shoots her twice. She drops. Both officers approach. The one who didn't fire kicks the saw away.

"Control. We have two down. Control?"

He looks at his companion: "No signal."

"Wait. Tom and Sienna will have heard the shots."

"Better." The voice is deep and slow.

Both men turn to point their guns at the woman.

"Give me your fires."

Her hands rise to meet the rushing warmth as both men shoot her, then stagger, eyes turning glassy.

Tom and Sienna come through the doors ready for anything. On seeing a woman with flames flickering from her eyes standing over the bodies of their teammates, they both open fire with compact assault rifles. The bullets flash as they strike her. Smoking holes appear in her clothing.

"Autofire!"

They both empty their clips into her. She steps backwards, stumbles over an outstretched arm, and falls.

"Changing."

Sienna slots a full clip into her assault rifle.

"Changing."

Tom pauses until she brings her assault rifle to bear, then reloads his. They advance with fingers on their triggers.

"Give me your fires."

As both of them twist and collapse, bullets spray the room.

PAR

We hear the wail and warble of alarms.

"Too late. Let's get quieter, and up to a higher vantage point."

Settling on a rooftop nearly opposite, we watch their response forces arrive.

"Red constructs?"

Pashta answers Liddy's question, and anticipates the next two.

"They bring water and equipment to fight the fires. The ones with green or red cross signs on them are healers. The yellow and blue ones are for civil loremen and lorewomen."

That's a little too simplified for anyone who's been here as long as Liddy, but she ignores the baiting and continues.

"The black one?"

Kon and I peer over the edge. He winks at me and replies in kind.

"It's that loreman without uniform and the loremistress he answers to. They have a new construct."

"Not that. *That.*" She points up, not down!

High above, there might be something? It's not black to me, but Liddy's perception of things unseen is so far beyond anything I've ever known, it's occasionally frightening.

Whatever that is, it's circling. It's something big, too. If I saw similar in the skies of Nethaly, I'd say it was a *drashen*-sized watcher construct... Which means this big something can likely *see us*.

"Down through this building into the underworld. Get gone!"

They go. I take a last look over the edge. The loreman without uniform is looking this way. That gives me an idea. I pull the wrap from my hand, wave to get his attention, then point up toward the big thing. I see him jerk in surprise. I give him what I hope is a 'thumbs up', then run like Shonnu is angry and on my tail. Which, it occurs to me, could be regarded as useful practice.

I wrap my hand again as I flee across a dozen rooftops before dropping down into a narrow alleyway. An access panel for their underground railway system lets me into the underworld, and I am free and away to fight in another affray.

FİVE

The alert comes when they're a kilometre out. Shots fired, officers down, fire, casualties. Three armed response units, two fire crews, one armoured paramedic truck and a mobile incident command already on the way.

"Damn it. If we'd been in my car that would have been priority routed to us."

Meredith activates lights and sirens.

"Flag us as attending."

Pete carefully taps in the correct code on the narrow screen set into the door at a perfect angle for someone to overconfidently type too fast. One character off and they'll be shown as attending a shoplifting or prostitution call. The prostitution one gets more laughs - from the other DCs, at least. Meredith hadn't found either mix-up amusing.

They arrive just behind the paramedics and park a way down the street to leave the access open. It also affords them a chance of departing when they want to, rather than having to wait for the inevitable emergency services car park to clear.

Pete gets out and looks about the scene. New Monument seems undisturbed, apart from the trickle of greasy smoke coming from between the front doors. No broken windows, no visible bodies.

He turns to Meredith: "We walking into a live scene?"

She shakes her head.

"The perpetrator is not considered to be in the vicinity. Put your headset on, Pete. I'm not your secretary."

He grins and does so, then spends a while quelling the holographic defaults and setting the eyescreen to deploy when tapped, not automatically on receipt of updates.

"That you, DC Reeves?"

"Yes. Who is this?"

"Operator Sixteen, currently in the back of the ARV to your far left. I have a flag for you from Traffic Team."

"Traffic? Is it flagged urgent?"

"No. Imperative."

"Okay, patch them through."

There's a moment of clicking before the link connects.

"Evening, DC Reeves. This is Constable Ruflin of Drone Unit Four. I have a sighting for you."

"Can it wait? We're on scene."

"So is this, sir. Your scene, too. That's why I routed it direct."

Pete looks about, snapping his fingers to get Meredith's attention.

"Tell me."

"One of our lowboy drones passed by about ten minutes ago. It picked up a cluster of visual anomalies on an opposite rooftop, three doors down-terrace from the entrance to New Monument Hospital."

Pete mentally works that out: left rear.

"They match the active visual cloaking you circulated a description of."

"Good work, Constable. Thank you. Reeves out."

He looks up, trying to appear like he's just looking about.

"Boss, we might have company."

"Where?"

"The sighting is ten minutes old. On the rooftop where I'm looking now... What the fuck?"

A hand appears, hanging in space, dark against clouds lit by sunset. He squints to try and make out a camouflaged arm, but the hand waves at him. Waves! Then points up? He peers. What could? There! He nearly loses sight of the high-flying object when the hand gives him an awkward thumbs up before snapping back out of sight.

"What did I miss?"

"Boss, either I'm losing it, or one of our quintet just deliberately caught my attention to point out the bloody great drone circling above us."

"Drone where?"

He points, bringing his phone to bear as well.

"Zoom to movement. Auto and identify."

The phone seeks, then beeps. He concentrates on holding it steady.

"Got it?"

"Think so. Phone should do the querying for us."

The phone starts giving details: "GA-ASI Avenger ER-B2. Receiving default reply to MetPol query: 'Operational details are restricted to MoD cleared personnel only'."

"What in the hell?"

"Seconded."

The phone continues: "Police challenge validated. Standing down."

They watch the huge drone become clearer against the sky above as it exits stealth mode. That done, it swings gracefully about and heads north, picking up speed as it goes.

Pete looks at Meredith.

"I retract my hasty assertation about this being a minor case. I also note that our very latest stealth, cloaking - or whatever it's called - technology is made to look stupid by whatever our quintet are using."

She nods: "Accepted and agreed. I'd give good odds that was monitoring this scene."

He waves a finger toward the rooftop.

"Curiously, so were they."

"A mystery for later."

"Give you that. Best we take a look at the scene before a horde of interested agencies interrupt in person because we made their drone pack up and go home in disgrace."

"Good idea. Follow my lead if I have to say anything outrageous."

"Noted."

KRO

She looks about, the fires that serve her for eyes lighting the darkness for a long way. She'd become accustomed to vermin fleeing her path, but no more. Now she stands in a smooth-cut tunnel, laid to loose stones set with great wooden battens to support the metal runners that go as far as she can see in either direction.

'Tube'?

Strange words keeping coming into mind without warning, always accompanied by confusing images. She doesn't care to understand either sending. This place should be a wasteland where the wailing essences of those cast out are left to drift without recourse. Somewhere they could lament the very thought of failing the desires of their Guthanes. A place so barren they would be eager to serve her for the remotest chance of gaining her favour, thinking her able to return them to their fanes.

Instead she finds some stinking metropolis, *and* is rescued by that insufferable *crepsty* Narbyl wearing new flesh! Still leading a warband! They're all rejects, but the purity of the insult is not mitigated. Worse still, that little *thaj* Liddy killed her! Her! How dare they turn on her! First, she must strengthen herself. *Lathny* doesn't work here, which is why her early attempts failed so miserably. In front of Narbyl, too! He'll pay for these slights. They all will.

Esseny is always present for those with the right. Lesser lives contributing to the causes of those greater. It is the very embodiment of the righteous path she has followed since before insipid, irritating Heklary raised her from portside fortune-teller to incarnate.

She needs essence. Eventually, it will come from a devoted host tithing to her. For now, any number of lesser lives to consume will suffice.

Bright light floods the tunnel. A noise like spears in flight, steppes wind and morning thunder shakes her. Her fires are torn free as the 18:16 from Warwick Avenue spreads her borrowed form across its front. Her legs kick once before being torn off.

Tina Straplin has never harboured any delusions about her weight. She's comfortable being a big woman. How dare the skinny freaks tell her how to live? Her doctor, she'll allow to lecture her, but the woman obviously has the time and money to go the gym every night on the way home. She might mean well, but she can't understand the needs that have to take priority for Tina.

Like being mugged while standing up for clothes to keep her son and daughter from being picked on by the spiteful little shits they share a school with. Even the rent has to wait for that.

A woman dressed in rags appears in the lights of the train. Tina hits the emergency brake. She knows there's no time to stop. She knows the woman is going to die. She sees the flaming eyes. She knows that she *must not* hit that thing, and that she cannot avoid it.

The train plows into the body. Two flaming orbs pass through the front of the cab and hover in front of Tina. Her breath catches. Her heart thumps so hard she expects it to fly from her chest. It doesn't. Nor does it beat further. Tina's hands ineffectually slap at the control boards, trying to hit the panic button. She swings an arm toward the door into the carriage. It never lands. She slides to the floor, gracelessly folding half-in, half-out of her seat.

Amber light throws flickering shadows on the wall through the windows of the driver's cab. Something screams and fades.

The passengers are still picking themselves up and wondering what caused the halt when the lights go out along the length of the train, darkness flickering like stop motion from carriage to carriage, starting at the rearmost. As the lights in the foremost go out, the cab door opens and fiery eyes throw dancing shadows from panicking people trying to escape.

"Give me your fires."

six

The reception is smoke-stained but free of other damage. Pete can see missing tiles where they'd filled the ceiling above. How does that damn gun of theirs do it? He can't get theories from experts in weapons or physics.

The stairs down to the mortuary are blackened. A fireman waits at the foot of the stairs. He smiles wide in greeting.

"DS Tanner. Whatever brings you here?"

"The smell. Reminds me of you, Crew Commander Andrews."

He recoils, then grins slightly less enthusiastically.

"I might have deserved some of that."

Meredith snorts.

"What are we about to walk in on?"

He grimaces.

"Nasty business. Two in the doorway, five on the floor of the room, two on a table, over a dozen pre-deceased corpses cooked in their drawers by the heat. Bullet holes all over the place. I've had to seal the whole wall with the drawers until we can secure and cool the scene enough to allow specialists in with the proper gear to deal with that. Be warned, out here might as well be a flower stall in comparison: it smells really awful in there. Don't hang about, and mind the hole in the floor."

Pete stops mid-stride and looks back.

"What hole?"

"Far side of the furthest support pillar. Just under a metre wide. Looks like someone took a thermic lance to the floor, went all the way down and through into the old tavern cellars. Hell of a job. Tidy as you like."

Meredith comes back to join Pete.

"Those cellars were blocked off as part of the foundation build, I presume?"

Andrews shrugs.

"Buildings regulations would have required it, and site inspection will have verified it. But, if it actually happened? That's a different thing altogether. A lot of alternative lifestyle types like room to run under the streets of our historic capital city, and some are prepared to pay handsomely for the privilege."

"As opposed to the ones that threaten to harm your family if you don't comply?"

"There was me trying to keep things upbeat. Yes, there are several criminal enterprises that occasionally like to have building plans run past them."

She looks at Pete.

He sighs: "We can assume the perpetrator escaped."

Meredith raises her hands in exasperation.

"Back to the station, then. The crime scene boys and girls can handle this. We'd only get in the way."

They're walking through reception when she gestures to the damage about them.

"Ever get the feeling we're playing bit parts in a drama we can't see?"

"Every damn day. Not sure it's all the same play, though."

"Oh, shut up."

"Can I dr-"

"Still 'no'."

ҐALA

Liddy skids to a stop, slime spraying from under her boots.

"She's flaring again."

Tarme frowns. The pale flame in his hand goes out. Pashta chuckles and manifests a replacement in her hand.

He smiles into the golden light.

"Always evening sunlight with you."

Pashta shrugs.

Liddy staggers a little, face going wan.

"Getting a lot stronger."

Tarme snaps his fingers to get Kon's attention, then tilts his head toward Liddy. Kon moves quickly to her side and encourages her to walk. That done, he glances at Tarme.

"She's killing, isn't she?"

He nods.

"Taking the essence of innocents."

"Narbyl's not going to like that." Pashta shakes her head sadly.

Liddy looks up.

"We'll have to stop him charging in. She's easily got more power than us. I thought the earlier flare-up was her topping up. I was wrong. She just didn't have many victims nearby."

Kon looks from Tarme to Pashta and back, his face ashen.

"How do we stop an angry, newbodied incarnate?"

Tarme sighs.

"A good question."

Liddy smiles, then nods.

"That Narbyl will be able to answer, if we can stop him killing himself by trying to be a noble *thaj* instead of the cunning *shemsil* we know he can be."

Kon grimaces: "Someone will have to force him to take the time to think. I lay first claim to not being that one."

They all chuckle as they plod and slide towards their fane.

SEVEN

They get the call while stuck in traffic on the way back to Druid's Hill. Meredith switches on the lights and sirens. When they fail to produce any reaction from the cars about them, she slaps the wheel in frustration.

"Some people."

Pete smiles: "Which is most of them when they're trying to get home."

She presses the 'priority traffic' button.

"We are not going to be popular."

"I asked them nicely."

She glares ahead.

"Why aren't they moving?"

Pete jumps: "I better flag us as attending. Give our priority routing a target."

Meredith lightly backhands his shoulder.

"You're right. It helps if the traffic-controlling monster knows where we need to go."

He taps it in.

Ahead of them, the traffic starts rearranging itself to create a passage for their car. They can see people angrily gesticulating and shouting.

"Nobody opening their windows to spit or throw things. That's nice."

She chuckles.

"Nice, nothing. The control package was amended in version 6.2: 'in addition to all doors being locked without override, any windows facing the prioritised route will also be closed and locked out. Use of both will be released to the occupants of the vehicle at the same time mobility priorities are restored'."

Pete coughs.

"I hope it also notifies Traffic about the vehicular chaos we're creating."

"It does. They assign a dedicated sub-team."

"So we get to be hated by the public and some of our colleagues?"

She looks at him.

"Did you know you're a pessimist?"

"Started after last year's salary review."

"Comments like that do not bode well for this year, either."

Pete points at the narrow strip of clear road.

"Pay attention, boss. An RTA on the way wouldn't look good, especially in this."

Meredith lifts her hands off the wheel.

"I'm only abiding by policy. An approved priority traffic routing puts these saloons into autodrive."

She puts her hands back.

"Pull up the incident details."

He does so. Seeing the size of the report, he pushes it from side display to main screen. It reformats itself so the driving details appear in a heads-up display on the windscreen in front of the driver's seat, while the incident details fill the dashboard screen from door to door.

"Ye gods."

He nods and opens the Incident Particulars tab.

"You got that right. Okay. The scene is the Bakerloo Line service from Paddington to Harrow and Wealdstone. The train left Warwick Avenue on time at 18:16. The incident stopped it midway between there and Maida Vale."

"Which part is the scene?"

Pete looks at her, voice going quiet: "The whole train."

She points at the comms feed window.

"Major incident just declared."

Her phone chimes. She looks puzzled.

"Which bit makes that noise?"

She looks. Her eyes narrow, then she laughs.

"Did you know our pretty handsets have a priority messaging app from GCHQ? I know that now because it's just informed me there is a Captain Mikhail Felowes from the MoD meeting us at the scene. Apparently, he has some urgent questions for us."

"Good thing too. The day was getting boring."

She tries to keep a straight face, but sputtering with laughter ruins it.

RAET

I try to stay calm, though every fibre of me screams for Liddy to
point the way so we can confront Shonnu before she kills again.
Through gritted teeth, I ask for confirmation.

"You are sure she is beyond us?"

Liddy drops, spins on her backside, and lies back so she can gaze
up into my eyes where I sit forward with my elbows on my knees,
staring at the floor.

"I'm getting bored of repeating myself. For the last time: right now,
she would consume us all. Ignore our attacks, burn us immobile, then
steal our flames. Look into my eyes. I'm not playing safe; I'm trying
to stop you getting us all killed for nothing."

"But-"

"Nothing, Narbyl. Right now, she will win, no matter what we do."

Thaj.

I lean back. They're all gathered about me. I check their spacing:
fight-ready in case I try to start something foolish. I make myself
take a deep breath. Make myself let it out slower than it came in. Do
it again. On the third attempt, I feel my tension ease a little. Right.
To the planning.

"Suggestions?"

They exchange glances. Pashta pulls Liddy up, then crouches at my side.

"We talked it over on the way back. The only being with experience of *esseny* is Gatchimak, and that is only if a couple of rumours Tarme heard are true."

I wave slowly at Kon, then grin.

He grins right back, makes an obscene sign at me, then heads for the computer in the corner.

Having got it going, he calls out: "Narbyl. You want him to come here?"

"Yes. Apologise for not abiding by courtesy, but we do not have the luxury of time to visit and petition him for aid."

I look at the rest of them.

"What do you think she'll do? Is there anything I've forgotten to deal with?"

Pashta rests a hand on my arm.

"You've not forgotten anything major lately. You seem to be better when there's a mission to brace your mind against."

Tarme stretches, joints clicking.

"She's right. As for Shonnu, I have no idea what the glut of power she took is for, but I believe she'll be looking to establish a fane. Somewhere she can be worshipped."

Liddy sits cross-legged, leaning back against Tarme's legs.

"I agree. I also think she'll be recruiting."

Tarme reaches down and ruffles her hair.

"The tiny storm is right, but not how she thinks. Reminds me a glut of power like that could be used to bind. After being delivered here, and getting killed by us, I don't think she'll be in a trusting frame of mind any more - if she ever had such a thing."

Pashta waggles her fingers at Liddy and Tarme while trying to put words to the realisation she's had.

"She'll take the choicest of those she felled. To make *Natrana*."

I rummage through this new language to find words that capture the nature of the affront she mentions. Nothing I can find fits. I give up and go with the literal translation.

"Mindless? You think she's creating Mindless?"

Pashta waves a hand in partial agreement.

"Whatever the *esseny* equivalent is."

Liddy grins.

"If I got closer, I could tell you."

Pashta slaps her calf.

"If you got close enough, Shonnu would consume you."

Liddy shrugs and winks at me: "Truth spoken."

Kon rejoins us and sits down next to Liddy.

He chuckles as he speaks.

"Gatchimak thinks you're an incorrigible upstart, but sadly agrees that manners must yield to expedience."

Pashta bursts out laughing.

"He used at least ten times as many words to say that, and was scornful of all of us along the way. Miserable, handsome *thaj* that he is."

Kon nods solemnly.

"You will never know. That man could talk rocks into pebbles."

I smile. Gatchimak may not be a Guthane anymore – and, as I now know, was only ever a Guthane by Heklary's gifting - but I count him a friend, for all that I let Kon do the talking.

"When will the former incarnate be joining us?"

"Tomorrow afternoon."

Good enough.

"Time to eat and sleep. Make both goodly, because we may not get a chance to settle for a while after tonight."

EİGHT

Sutherland Avenue is in chaos. The rather pleasant residential street has parking at kerbs and either side of the central reservation. The arrival of a major incident response has effectively blocked the road in both directions for the foreseeable future.

"Why are we descending on suburbia?"

Meredith points toward the crane deploying at the end of the road, just this side of the roundabout.

"There's an old freight-lift shaft that was paved over, leaving a maintenance panel for engineering access. By some sad luck, the front of the train is right under it. We've received perm-"

She glares at Pete.

"Put your bloody headset on."

"Two and a half sentences this time."

"I'll put them on your headstone if you don't stop this game."

"Still say you'd make a great secretary."

"Something I kept telling her, but she was determined to be a bloody detective."

They both jump. Pete's eyes widen.

"Good evening, ma'am."

Meredith grins.

"Hello, mum."

Pete's mouth drops open.

"DC Peter Reeves. A pleasure to meet my daughter's favourite topic of irritation at last. I'm Commissioner Kathleen Burns. Merry insists on using her father's surname to ensure no taint travels either way."

Pete snaps his mouth shut.

"Either it's worked, or I'm the last ignoramus left standing. Ma'am."

She laughs.

"You're genuinely funny. Refreshing, and that's this relaxing interlude over. Your Captain Felowes from the Ministry of dodging questions is waiting in the grey tent a little way behind you. After that, there's a horror show down below that I have been instructed by senior members of said Ministry to leave completely alone until you two have seen it. So, please, get a bloody move on."

Kathleen spins on her heel and walks away.

Meredith coughs: "She's furious. At home, she'd be spitting and swearing."

He nods toward the grey tent: "Game on?"

"Yes. Let's not be hanging about, either."

They walk quickly.

"Merry?"

She scowls.

"You want a marble or granite headstone?"

"Noted, boss."

Inside the tent is the tallest man Pete has ever met.

As he shakes Meredith's hand, he nods to Pete.

"Two point one metres is the answer to that, DC Reeves."

Pete chuckles.

"Establishing your keen observational skills and inferring operational oversight, while throwing the pair of us off our stride. Also subtly insulting my Detective Sergeant by not introducing yourself while shaking her hand. So, apart from playground tricks and being fucking rude, what use are you?"

He finishes his summation staring the man straight in the eyes.

The officer smiles and ducks his head, trying to hide his eyes narrowing in anger.

"None at all, from your point of view. But, to honour your rebuke, I'll cut to the chase and get myself out of your way."

Meredith bursts out laughing.

"Okay, penis lengths duly noted. Captain, you have questions?"

"I want to know what you know about our AWOL Avenger." He blinks.

Pete grins. She winks at him.

"Your GA-ASI Avenger drone? We spotted it circling above us while attending a crime scene and fire in the mortuary of New Monument Hospital earlier today. When DC Reeves queried it with his official phone, it invoked MoD-level non-disclosure, dropped stealth, and headed north. RTB, we presumed."

The Captain looks thoughtful. He whispers: "Putting its toys away, again."

Meredith softly whispers: "Again?"

"Our ghost always returns what it borr- Oh, you two are good."

He pauses to brush imaginary specks off dust off his shoulder while he gathers himself.

"I think I've dropped myself quite deep enough in it without going for an encore. Please excuse me."

He steps between them and leaves. They're looking at each other, trying to find words, when he sticks his head back into the tent.

"There's a ghost in the machine. It's untraceable, but seems to be interested in you. If you find out anything, please call the MoD and ask for me. Good luck."

The head withdraws.

Meredith aims a rude gesture after him, then grins at Pete. He looks thoughtful, then chuckles.

"Rinsed him good."

"That was fun, if confusing."

"True. Now for the main event."

The seven-carriage tube train had been packed with commuters. Most of them are still there, lying three and four deep, eyes glassy, bodies cold.

"This is. Is…" Pete's voice tails off. How do you encompass this?

"No words?"

"That too."

Meredith swallows slowly. Of all things, it's the lack of soiling that gets to her. Nobody seems to have passed anything on dying. For the number of deaths, it's unheard of.

Pete looks about.

"They were running from something. It came at them from the front of the train."

She shines her light toward the front of the train, seven carriage lengths away.

"The only blood is back here. Six carriages and there's no sign of violence, just dead people who were killed trying to get away from something. Probably the something that killed them."

He steps next to her and shines his torch the other way.

"Still trying to get past the disturbing thought of a thing so terrifying people would ignore the approach of certain death to try and escape it instead... They were fighting to get out. After running the length of the train, they met the wall at the end. The desperation to escape drove someone to put a window out."

"Scene info states they used a pair of folding pushbikes and brute force."

"It was the right thing to do, but it set off a stampede. Everyone wanted out. That's when the bloodshed started. People tearing at each other.

"Get uniforms to check the survivors and their effects. I see stab wounds as well as roughhousing. At least one person used a knife to improve their chances."

He points to a body draped over a chair.

"That wound to his temple? Someone used a medium size angle piton like a punch dagger. Expect to find a few more injuries like that."

Dropping into a crouch, he examines a woman in a business suit crumpled against the wall under the smashed window.

"She would have made it, except someone put a screwdriver or similar into her back. Punctured a lung, at a guess."

He stands up.

"How many?"

"Accurate numbers won't be available until tomorrow at the earliest. It'll be somewhere between four and five hundred."

"On *one* train?"

She checks her phone: "The Bakerloo line was designated a heritage track a decade ago. These are the original 1972 rolling stock with extensive refurbishment. Peak capacity for a seven-carriage unit was originally 847. Refurbishment and new regulations reduced it to 707. At the time of night it ran, usage would have been around seventy percent. That's 494 people, plus the driver. Current estimates are that sixty people escaped."

Pete steadies himself against a seating rail. There's a bloody handprint next to his gloved hand. It's barely half the size of it.

"Please tell me the kids got out."

Meredith checks.

"Remote scanning has all the fatalities as adults. I'm showing one ten-year-old with a broken wrist." She looks at Pete: "No deaths."

He sighs.

"Some orphaned, though, I'd bet. Thinking further, that I'll allow: using a blade to get your kid to safety when the panicked masses won't budge."

Meredith gestures toward the ladder propped against the open door.

"We're done here."

He shakes his head.

"No, we're not."

Pete heads back up the train. She hesitates, then follows him. He never wastes time at a scene, so he must have spotted something.

"How long ago did this happen?"

"Three hours, give or take a half hour."

He points his phone at a body.

"Diagnostic. Cadaver, human, death point 195 minutes."

The phone beeps twice. A minute or so later, it beeps once.

"Body temperature conflicts with death point estimation. Please hold unit in clear space at least two metres from any cadaver for ambient temperature determination."

Pete does so.

"Please return phone to scan the same cadaver."

Meredith watches Pete watching his phone, seemingly unaware he's quietly counting seconds.

"Body temperature anomaly. It is cooler than the ambient temperature. Ambient temperature is sixteen degrees. Cadaver is at eight degrees."

"End diagnostic."

He slips the phone back into its holster.

"Something's very, very off, boss." He looks about. "Let's get out of here."

Above ground, after quaffing two strong teas while sharing a soggy cheese and pickle sandwich, they step up into the back of an ambulance and sit across from a small, heavily bandaged, woman.

Meredith smiles: "Miss Gwon? You insisted on seeing us?"

She tries to smile back, shudders, and waves a hand resignedly. Bandages, pads and surgical tape cover the right side of her head. The left side is dark with bruises. Her voice is slurred.

"Forgive. My face is a mess. Thank you for coming quickly. I'd like to get the criminal side settled before my family arrive."

Pete exchanges a puzzled glance with Meredith.

"Criminal, Miss Gwon? Why don't you take us through it all from the start, so we can get the full picture, then we can go from there."

"Please, call me Annika. I was late leaving the office, managed to squeeze onto the train at Embankment. I finally managed to get a seat at Regent's Park.

"The train came to a hard stop. I was facing backwards, so the seat held me up, but the man opposite got thrown into me. I think the edge of his laptop broke a rib."

Pete taps to deploy his eyescreen. He's just in time to catch Meredith's update.

> Diagnosis confirms two broken ribs.

"What happened next, Annika?"

"The lights went out. There were a couple of screams. A man swore loudly. The chap in my lap got up and used his phone to find his seat. The little lights above the doors at either end came on.

"We just sat there. There was a bit of banter, but most people stayed engaged with their devices. It must have been ten, maybe fifteen minutes before I heard a commotion coming from the next carriage. Some people near the connecting door got up and moved past me towards the back of the train. I saw a couple of big men pick up folding bicycles. I wouldn't have noticed, but a smaller man in cycling gear complained. One of the men told him 'need something to crack out, you can have it back'. I heard them getting people to move, heard them start hitting a window somewhere behind me. Then the door at the other end crashed opened and people came pouring in, screaming, shouting, crying. They were climbing over each other! The noise was awful.

"I got up and moved round to join the two big men. They were really giving that window a beating. More people were coming down the carriage, there didn't seem to be an end to them. They were panicky, running. One woman went past all of us and ran straight into the door to the driver's section at the back. She picked herself up, then started banging on the door.

"The biggest of the two men said something obscene, backed across the carriage, flattened himself against the opposite window, then put one foot against the wall underneath. With a shout, he launched himself at the window they'd been working on. Hit it flat out. The window gave, shattered with a horrendous noise. He disappeared off the train. His friend jumped out right after. I managed one step to follow them before the man who had landed on me shoved his hand up my skirt! I though he was trying it on, but he just lifted and threw me toward the passengers coming down the carriage. I hit some of them and fell down. I remembered what my mother said about accidents in the Seoul Metro and pulled myself under a seat before I got trampled.

"By this time, there were people everywhere. I've never seen anything like it. The noise had changed. It was like one animal, high-pitched roar. People were getting stamped on, getting really hurt. I slid over by a window, dragged myself upright, then stayed flat against the windows and squeezed toward that only way out. People were hitting my back as they fought, I lost my coat because someone wouldn't let go of it. My blouse got torn to bits. By the time I made it to the broken window, I wasn't in my right mind. That's the only excuse I have."

"For what, Annika?"

"That man. The one in the blue sweatshirt. He stabbed me! The pain was so sharp, I just reacted – I trained in Seoul for years. Broke his wrist, pulled the dagger out of my side, shoved it into him. He punched me through the window as I did that. I went out backwards, half turned, and hit the ground face first."

She gestures to her bandaged face: "They say it'll be fine after some surgery."

"You came down that hard?" Meredith sounds surprised.

Annika half-smiles.

"No. Someone escaping the train landed with one knee on my head. After that, my memory gets a bit confused."

"Did you see what everyone was trying to get away from?"

She shakes her head.

"All I saw?" She pauses, visible eye narrowing.

"It looked like someone was waving orange torches about?"

Pete glances at Meredith. She tilts her head toward the doors they came through.

"Thank you, Annika. We'll let the ambulance take you now. Don't worry about the criminal thing. It was clearly self-defence, on top of being in the midst of an emergency."

She looks relieved.

They exit the ambulance and walk slowly back toward the saloon.

"This, to borrow a favourite term of my mother's, is somewhat fucked up."

"And then some, boss. What now?"

"I don't think we can do anything useful here or at the office. Clock off, get sorted, get fed, and please get some sleep instead of playing guitar. The way things are going, tomorrow could be a very long day and I'll need you on form."

"Yes boss." He looks at their blocked-in car. "I'll get a lift from one of the patrol boys. G'night."

"Goodnight, Pete."

She gazes at the double row of vehicles between the saloon and the road home. With a resigned sigh, she looks about, then whispers into the night: "More than somewhat fucked up."

CRⱯII

My sensitivity to *lathny* and *esseny* has saved me, and those who look to me, many times. Since I first woke here, my ability has been next to useless.

Tarme says that, on top of a problem with my mind, the amount of copper in use all about us means there is always a constant level of what sensitivity like mine interprets as *lathny*.

I'm awake. Fully roused, fight ready, alert. *Esseny*. Nearby, very strong.

"Gatchimak, you *thaj*. Ease it off."

"Uncle Gatch said you'd feel it before I put you to sleep. Greetings, *shemsil* Narbyl. I'm Tershyp. I didn't get a chance to be polite after you rescued me."

I lever my upper body off the sleeping pad and look in the direction of the voice, swinging my arms round, blade and suppressor wand ready.

She makes a little surprised noise.

"You have moments to release my companions from your meddling."

I raise my gaze to find a pinkish lattice floating in front of her eyes.

"Not yet. Uncle Gatch gave me a message for you alone."

"Speak."

"'In this place of our joyous exile, Shonnu is unprecedented. Some here have weapons of such power that I can barely grasp their nature. Without any insult intended: you could not comprehend them.

"'Simply be sure that should Shonnu manifest anywhere the holders of those weapons can get an inkling as to what she could do, they will eventually panic and use their terrible arsenal. The entirety of this vast island we make our fanes upon will be laid low in such a way that not even grass will survive. Believe this. Let it influence your plans.

"'Lastly, I ask that you let my adopted daughter aid you.'"

She sighs: "He said I have far greater ability in the things you need."

I smile at her, dropping my wand and making my blade disappear. She tilts her head.

"You didn't use *lathny* or *esseny*."

I reappear the blade, then turn my hand and arm over before showing her the move again. She moves her arm and hand in clumsy imitation.

"I'll practice, but be useless for ages."

"As was I. Spent many a morning cleaning clothes for my failures, too. You can skip that bit, if you like."

She laughs.

"Yes please, *shemsil*."

I raise a hand: "Call me Narbyl. We're a long way from anywhere that title has meaning."

"As you instruct."

I stop getting out of bed and stare at her.

"Gatchimak told you to use those words at some point, didn't he?" She grins.

"Said I might learn a new curse or two if I did."

From the old me, certainly.

"Used to be true. Now, here's how it goes: new world, new language, need to fit in. Our bodies allow us to translate, but it's literal, which is not always fitting. That's when we use Nethalyn: when there are no words in this language that fit. But, even then, the preference should be to always use this tongue, no matter how silly the new words seem. We frequently understand, anyway. Like we can back-translate to the spirit of the words."

"What about '*thaj*'?"

"I have heard people here cursing in what I presume are their home tongues, yet conversing in this one." I shrug, then grin: "Plus, if there's a need to use it, I'm past caring about translation."

"I can understand that. Shall I wake the others?"

"Release them, but don't jog them. Practice your patterns, starting with the least. Let's see who feels you and who has to be woken."

I watch her weave wonders and nightmares from pink light. It reminds me of something here. What is that? Neon! That's it.

I look at her. She looks like a native. For all that we wear bodies left behind when their essences departed, our essences always subtly change them. Enough to seem strange in some way to those born here. Enough to pass for someone who only *looks* like a dead relative so recently lost. Absolute truth, a grievous lie, and a walking second chance for each of us exiles.

What started the expulsion cult had already been lost by the time I was born. It was used as an ultimate punishment, taking several loreweavers from Kethany to weave the expulsion construct the guilty one was clamped into.

Some subsections of the urban dwellers imitated those constructs for decadent purpose. Out in the wilds such aberration simply told us the metropolis cults were failing: reduced to artless mimicry.

After all the time I've had to think on it since being subjected to it, I still have to presume the newbody phenomenon is unknown to those who use expulsion.

It's meant to be the worst way to die. While I understand many on Nethaly, and all from Kethany, would look upon the mundane existences here with horror, it's hardly an eternal punishment. The newbody we get seems to be a chance thing outside of gender and size, although physical abilities can be a rough match to what we had - given enough training. The newbody comes with any limitations it had prior to the original death, although the killing injury is healed or removed. The mind inside provides what I presume is the facility for language of the original, plus a random selection of memories, all of them with one or more associated images, and every memory unknown to the exile until it's invoked by some event or sighting. It can be disconcerting, especially if intimate memories surface when you're trying to focus on something important – or in my case, just focus.

Tershyp continues weaving wonders, intricate braids of muted light and suspended dark. I catch the glint of a pair of eyes reflecting her lights. Tarme gives me the slightest nod. He's watching her. She hasn't spotted him.

Spotting exiles was a waking nightmare until Liddy was delivered. Edrie and Seemu would spend hours poring over this place's news journals. Nothing as simple as Nethaly and Kethany, where the journals we referred to were limited to one for each of the Guthanes. Here it is a like a great lake filled with news fish. Some are easy to catch. Some want to catch you. Many are poisonous, many are lies, some are both. Others are difficult to catch. They might be lies, too. But you have to try, just in case. It's maddening.

I don't know how those two managed it. I would have asked, but the raid after the one that secured Liddy was the one in which Edrie was hit by a truck. Before we could gather, Seemu picked his body up and leapt off the edge of the mountain road, his love cradled in his arms.

One part of me mourns the loss of a bond like they shared. Another rages that a chance encounter could deprive us of two precious lives.

Liddy tells me whenever we lose a newbody we rescued. Once she's detected one, she can find it from that day forth. We're down to sixteen from forty. Of those, we five, Gatchimak, and through him Tershyp, are the only ones who stayed in contact. I wonder how many more of us there are. The expulsion cult would have started delivering essences to this world around the middle of the fifteenth century, as far as Tarme and Pashta can work out. Apart from a short hiatus while a redemption cult rose, flourished, and fell apart in bloody strife, expulsions happened more often than any were truly happy about. Power should be elegant and egalitarian, be it creating

safety, enforcing lore, or waging war. Expulsion is far from elegant.
Tarme says even the weavings that enable it are artless.

"Pretty lights. *Whup!* Welcome back, Tershyp!"

Liddy's up... Three, two, one.

"Kon!"

"Wha-ooof!"

That must have hurt.

"Will you two turn it down? Tarme, the lights are very nice and all
that but-" Pashta sits bolt upright, complaint forgotten: "Guthane of
Shadow! How are you weaving *lathny* and *esseny* without bleeding
everywhere, girl?"

I step out next to Tershyp.

"You can stop now, Weaver."

She blushes as the lights fade away.

Pashta's nodding.

"Truth spoken, Narbyl. That's going to complicate things."

Tarme bursts out laughing.

"Not at all. You can instruct her first. Complication removed."

Tershyp shakes her head.

"No, thank you. There's an old Weaver essence bound to a
decaying newbody buried in the graveyard near our fane. She's
lovely and I have a lot more to learn from her. We're running out of
time. She's fading."

I wave a finger at Tarme, my memory laughing as it evades me.

"Only one. Ever. Only one. I knew her granddaughter! Damn this
patchwork recall."

Tershyp leans over and catches my finger.

"Karadey Icefane."

I look into her eyes.

"She's named you, hasn't she?"

She looks at the floor, then whispers: "Only because you ask it."

Squaring her shoulders, she raises her head and looks across the room, eyes on none of us.

"Tershyp Karadey."

As she says it, a shower of ice crystals fall about her, flash blue, and are gone.

Tarme rises and bows to her.

"I acknowledge you, Weaver Child."

He looks to Pashta. She's crying. A golden halo forms about her head. She goes down on one knee.

"Steyl Ruinfane told me I would live to witness a Child in her name. Be twice acknowledged."

The halo fades: a telling redeemed.

Thaj.

In a world where powers seen and unseen could work together, I was surprised to find the idea of inheritance between Weavers was viewed very dimly. It was rumoured to have something to do with a potential to eventually threaten the power of incarnates. Now I know there was a difference between an incarnate and a Guthane, I get an inkling of the potential of natural power as opposed to those imbued – and of the lies used to prevent that ever being realised.

Wait a moment. Imbued? Like constructs? I need to mention that to Tarme sometime. Hold that instant, too. Pashta had been told she would live to see this come to pass?

Tarme has arrived by my side while I process things badly.

"I'll keep Pashta hale. Liddy and Kon will look to Tershyp. Your task is to turn this raiding party into a Guthane killer."

I rest a hand on his shoulder.

"Thank you for your confidence."

"You fail; we die. Therefore... Don't fail." He flashes me a grin.

I chuckle.

"Tershyp, for all that it's a paltry follow-up, tell us what Gatchimak has to say of Shonnu."

She nods, stealing a sip from Liddy's mug before starting.

"It's not much. He rambled on for a long while. I told him I couldn't remember it all and why didn't he email it to Kon? He shook himself like a bear coming out of the Maiallan Falls, then told me to tell you all this –

"'Shonnu is as near to a manifestation of the fire that destroys as was ever conceived of on Nethaly or Kethany. Heklary was often chided by the other Guthanes for creating something so dangerous.

"'Like fire, she is changeable - but always deadly. Like fire, she is devoid of strategy. Like fire, she has no restraint. Unlike fire, she is convinced of her right to rule. The latter two may be her only weaknesses.'"

Kon leans forward.

"Why am I less scared of doing something as stupid as fighting a mad incarnate than I was doing any of the stupid things I did on Nethaly, including the escapade that got me delivered here?"

Liddy reaches back and pats the outside of his thigh.

"Because you're with us, and together, led by Narbyl, we can easily out-mad Shonnu."

Tarme howls with laughter.

That's never happened before.

After a while, he looks across at me, tears rolling down his face.

"New strategy, *shemsil.* All you have to do is find something so crazy she won't expect it."

He has a point.

"Shouldn't be hard. All I have to do is work out the one attack that is crazy enough to surprise her, deadly enough to kill her, and selective enough not to kill us."

Everyone goes quiet.

Pashta rests a hand on Tershyp's knee.

"I think we all know that isn't likely. I say as long as Shonnu is obliterated and Tershyp makes it back to Gatchimak, it's a victory I will fight for."

One by one, they nod to me.

I look at Tershyp. She's smiling, but I see tears brimming.

"I will never accept dying as a part of victory, unless it is the only way. Take our Weaver out to get to know this metropolis that will likely be our battleground. I need to get to the planning."

Brave words. Can I manifest them into anything we have some small chance of surviving?

Thaj.

ΠİΠE

Meredith arrives early, despite having spent a restless night, even after the added exercise of finally escaping the scene by simply walking home. She'd left the saloon in autodrive, with a pending instruction to return to the charging bays in the garage below when a route cleared.

"Morning, boss. Coffee and a bagel on your desk."

She jumps as Pete wanders out from the break room to stand next to her.

"Did you actually make it home?"

"Sadly, yes. My neighbours' divorce is going very badly. She thinks he should shower more often. He thinks she should move in with her 'limp-wristed ladyboy' and leave him to his Pornstation and women who are honest enough charge up front. I decided to get a head start here before I became privy to any more details."

"They do know you're a police officer, don't they?"

"Yes. Apparently I'm 'as fake as the padding in her bra'." He shrugs: "Another snippet from the soap opera next door."

She chuckles.

"So, what has your predawn start got us?"

Pete smiles.

"I'm ghost hunting while waiting for the rest of the witness statements to come in."

"Speaking of ghosts, horrible as the link is: what are the numbers from the train?"

"405 dead. 64 survivors. 11 missing, including the driver: a long-term employee. Popular lady, by all accounts. Union rep, too. All the other missing are men between the ages of twenty and thirty.

"Of the survivors, only nine are uninjured. One of those has been arrested as he had a concealed knife that matches several of the injuries found on both survivors and deceased. Two others are the big lads Annika spoke of. They pretty much confirmed the view she gave us. We've also found the man in the blue sweatshirt, complete with a broken wrist and an antique dagger hilt-deep in his upper chest. Went clean through his left sub-clavicular artery."

"That is one tough lady."

"Agreed. I pushed through a special request on the bodies and have confirmed that 366 were abnormally cool, and – so far – none of those show visible causes of death."

"Ye gods. 39 died fighting to get off the train?"

"I'm favouring only 29 dying while trying to get off the train, no fighting involved per se. The other 10 might have had something to do with some of the fatalities, including each other's. They discovered a stray dagger on the floor in the last carriage, but are waiting for fingerprint matching to find the owner, deceased or otherwise.

"From my view, up to a dozen of the survivors also have deliberate, if not premeditated, blood on their hands. I've started enquiries on that basis. Especially to find the miserable bugger who put a screwdriver into the back of that woman when she was so close to escaping."

"I had a nightmare about the piton."

"We've got the superstar who pulled that. His girlfriend dumped him, then turned him in. She's at a station across town recording her statement right now."

"If she's a survivor, why isn't she here?"

"She's not. Like I said, 'superstar'. He was videoing himself from the moment he decided to get busy with the piton. Tried to impress her: she threw up. Uniforms have secured bodycam, hard drive, and piton. The video shows two other attacks, the last of them after getting off the train!"

"Another maniac revealed by a tragedy. That's above and beyond savage."

"No disagreement from this cheap seat, boss."

She wanders into her office, grabs coffee and bagel, then returns to his desk. Hooking herself a chair from across the way, she sits down.

"Okay. Talk to me about ghosts in the machine."

"'Ghost'. Singular."

"Sure about that?"

He ignores her and spends a couple of minutes dragging windows around his multi-screen setup.

"So: we are told we have an unidentified fan. What is certain is that fan is capable of hijacking a state-of-the-art military drone and spending a while gadding about above London without any interference. Which tells us said fan is good enough to avoid what we can presume to have been some fairly strenuous attempts to stop, find or kill them. I'm certain our fan has done this *many* times before. The equipment, nature, and duration of the borrowings are unavailable to us, but they've occurred often enough to establish an MO solid enough for dedicated MoD resources to be assigned."

Meredith grins round her coffee cup: "'Borrowings'. Like it." She raises the little finger on the hand holding her coffee: "I'd add that Captain Felowes initially thought we might be connected in some way. Having revised his opinion, he ducked out, but only after cueing us up."

Pete smiles.

"Good point. He's set us pedigree detective hounds on the trail, hoping we'll scare something from cover."

His screens go dark. Words appear.

You don't need to.

Pete stands up and looks about the office.

"Whoever this is, it's not fucking funny."

The words change.

Correct. London is in grave danger.

Meredith leans forward.

"Okay, I'll play. What from? When? How do you know this? Who the bloody hell are you? Why can't you stop it?"

A danger like nothing you have ever faced before.

Within a week.

I know what she's like.

My name is Heklary.

I'm dead.

Meredith spits coffee.

"What?"

That's why I need your help.

Other loremen are coming. I will talk to you soon.

The screens return to the displays Pete had so carefully organised. Detectives Leffer and Park amble in. They look startled to see the two of them already in the office.

"My office. Now."

Pete grabs his bacon bap and coffee. Entering her office, he heels the door closed and squeezes round the desk to take the other seat. She activates the office's privacy mode.

"What the fuck just happened?"

He waves both mug and bap helplessly.

"You were right there with me, boss. I have no fucking clue either."

She takes a deep breath.

"I'm sure there's no trace of what we just saw."

Pete puts both drink and food on the floor, then grabs the tablet from her desk and starts frantically flicking through options. A minute or so passes.

"Gotcha!"

He angles the pad so she can see the video feed montage from the office monitoring cameras as well. They appear in the lower left section. His screens and the words are clearly visible. She whoops.

"Yes!"

The screen goes black.

No.

Drive the same new vehicle you drove yesterday.

The video comes back, showing the two of them reviewing his displays – just like they never did.

"Am I alone in getting an eerie feeling from this spooky hacking show?"

Meredith presses her fingers on the back of his hand, then returns them to pick up her bagel.

"Proper horror movie chills. Something here is significantly out of kilter."

She takes a bite.

Pete reaches down, grabs his coffee and bap, takes a mouthful and looks across the desk at her, a grin forming on his face as he chews.

"We going for a drive?"

She swallows, then reaches for her coffee.

"Damn right."

The cup pauses before it touches her lips.

She grins: "No, you can't."

"Oh, come *on*."

KADA

Breaking fast with Tershyp and Liddy doing the preparation makes the whole affair boisterous. Seeing everyone's smiling faces at the tables is refreshing. Too often of late our mornings have been muted affairs as we contemplate our dwindling numbers and uncertain future.

"Hey, Narbyl."

I look up. Liddy grins, waving what looks like an iced *lakso* on the end of a- a- a... Fork! That implement is a *fork*. A spoon is a shallow scoop. A *spork* is not as good as either. Which is true of so many compromises.

Liddy points to Tershyp.

"Easy icing things with her here. I remembered Pashta said you liked this. Somewhere between the two made me think: why don't we ice Shonnu up? She's fire. Hot versus cold. We'd need a lot of ice, but surely this world has things that can make a lot of cold?"

In the sudden silence, the sound of Tarme's spoon hitting the floor is comically loud. Kon chuckles.

"Like lightning in all things."

Liddy sticks her tongue out at him: "That's not what you said last night."

Kon blushes. Tershyp chokes on her *lakso*.

"Change the subject. Narbyl's getting jealous." Pashta grins at me.

Liddy glances at me. Her eyes go wide. She flushes slowly from neck to nose. Oh, no. Better yet: never to be explored. It would be the death of me - either because of it, or because she will kill me for having the arrogance to think it possible.

"I was just thinking Kon may be brave in unappreciated ways."

The laughter is good. Pashta takes the iced *lakso* from Liddy and presents it to me with a little flourish.

I gaze at it. I used to love this. I wonder if it tastes the same with a new tongue? While I wait for it to thaw a little, I turn it slowly back and forth.

Iced incarnate. Well, why not?

TEⅡ

The garage is all but deserted. A pair of mechanics give them a wave from where they work on an ARV, standing on its roof to reach the second engine, which has been hoisted clear for some reason.

"Now that's a job stream I never understood the appeal of."

Meredith nods.

"Too busy trying to become a rock star, eh?"

"That was just to annoy my family. I always wanted to fly space shuttles."

She stops and stares at him.

"You're terrified of heights."

He spreads his hands.

"Then there's that. Thought I'd grow out of it."

"Bet it hurt when you realised."

Pete sighs.

"Joined the police to ease my suffering."

She snorts.

"Get in the car, you fool."

They stop either side of the saloon, each with one hand on the roof, the other on a door. They gaze at each other. Pete breaks the silence.

"You got that 'irrevocable' feeling too?"

She nods.

"Well, we can always resile and call the Captain. Or Mummy. Or both, then watch them fight over it."

"Take my mind off coming round there and hitting you by telling me what 'resile' means."

"'To draw back or recoil'."

"You phrased that sentence deliberately, didn't you?"

"To distract you from worrying over the piece of career-ending stupidity we're about to engage in? Yes."

"We have nothing to go on. Our five remain as elusive as ever. There is no trace of a perpetrator in the train attack. My use of the word 'attack' is being challenged. 'Unexplained incident' is now the preferred term. Did you browse the witness statements? 'Halloween mask', 'scary holograms', 'alien with lasers for eyes'-"

"I quite liked that one."

"'whispering shadows', 'she asked for a light', 'flaming-eyed raksheshi'..."

She stops.

"What is a 'raksheshi', anyway?"

"Female flesh-eating demon in physical form. Mentioned in Hindu and Buddhist mythology."

"You didn't even have to look that up, did you?"

"Would you think less of me if I said not?"

Meredith bursts out laughing.

"Okay, I feel a little better. Let's go."

They sit in the saloon. The glassy black dashboard reflects their faces.

Pete points at the ignition.

"You turn that, we're colluding with a national security threat."

"I've seen no Orange Notice from Interpol or the NCA."

"I don't think they want our fan's activities to be private information, let alone public. Trust me, we're about to step off the blue side."

She leans back.

"Something about this scares me. I can't pin it down, but there's too much unexplained about the body snatching, let alone the events of the last day. The whole case didn't make sense before, anyway, even from any of the insane rationales we could link, however tenuously. As for DS Stephen's idea about contagious copycat behaviour, don't get me started."

"He's an idiot, boss. You can ignore him. Besides, the case only gets worse if some of my possible thefts of other bodies turn out to be actual crimes. He wouldn't consider any of them."

Pete fiddles with his phone: "I want to find out what's going on, but I'm really, really not liking the sudden swerve this seems to have taken."

"No disagreement from the driver's seat, DC. So, we are left with two options that lead to known and unknown situations. We can get out of this car, go upstairs, and investigate further, likely getting nowhere until the train attack is soft-pedalled as a freak accident. The body snatching case will weigh us down for the next however long it remains open. Maybe we call the Commissioner. We could call the Captain – if the Commissioner agrees. What we tell either or both, I'm frankly at a loss over."

"The other simple option?"

"We drive out of here and who knows what the bloody hell will happen?"

Her phone beeps. She checks it.

"Scenes of crime have completed mapping. Apparently, there is a trail of scorch marks, melted materials, and incinerated vermin. It leads from the point the tube train impacted a body and stopped, all the way back to the derelict cellars under the New Monument mortuary. The body has been identified from tattoos on the severed limbs as that of senior morgue technician Reina Sambor."

She stares at him, eyes gone wide. His are wider. He points to the ignition.

"Start the car."

She does so. They exit the garage and turn toward New Monument Hospital.

"What now, boss?"

"I'll head for the old North Circular. If nothing happens, we'll get to see the old South Circular as well. After that, we get fish and chips. If we finish them without anything peculiar happening, I say we give up, come back here tomorrow and get on with normal police work like we're meant to be doing right now."

They drive in silence for nearly an hour. Without warning, the steering wheel retracts as the saloon enters full autodrive mode. The dashboard screen goes black.

Pete whispers: "Game on."

You are being followed by one car and one drone.

They are both approaching.

Please place your handsets in the cradles on the centre console.

Both their phones beep. The displays flash yellow and blue.

Both of these are monitored units.
You will need to reset them after this.

Pete shakes his head.
"No surprises there, then. Use 017700 698 2438."

That unit is off.

"So you can't turn it on?"

That is beyond me.
I need a single construct, and for that construct to be active.

"What happens when the unit is turned on?"

We can converse further.

The steering wheel unfolds. After Meredith has placed her hands on it, the car exits autodrive. He reaches out and starts the resets on both phones.

She points to the narrow screen set into his passenger door.

"Flag us as returning to Druid's Hill for diagnostics due to an unrequested engagement of fully autonomous autodrive."

"Clever."

Standing in the garage, they watch the technicians running checks. Pete turns about so they're watching in both directions. He waves a hand back toward the saloon.

"There isn't going to be any trace, is there?"

She shakes her head.

"Not a chance."

"What now?"

Meredith shrugs. Her phone rings.

"DS Tanner."

He sees her look of surprise.

"Yes, Commissioner."

She holsters her phone.

"Did you pack your manners this morning?"

Pete turns to face her.

"Why?"

"Because mummy wants me to bring you round for tea."

"She what?"

"Actually, she ordered the both of us to attend, but your expression is funnier this way."

"Not funny, boss."

"Not for you, maybe. All of a sudden, I need all the laughs I can get."

"Noted."

He gestures around the garage.

"You want to call for another super saloon or are we taking a vintage classic from the unmarked car pool?"

"She's sending a car."

His bantering expression vanishes. He frowns.

"This has just gone sideways, hasn't it?"

"Somehow, yes."

KİTHİ

After dedicating a morning to running through all the combat patterns I can remember, backwards, I allow myself a leisurely bath.

Returning to the main room, intending to eat, Kon interrupts me.

He beckons me over to show off something on the little window in front of him. He seems pleased with himself. I can't work out why.

"What is that?"

I hate these constructs called computers. So many words and pictures. So little substance. Kon says I'm missing the point. Tarme says I'm pure soldier.

"Lots of cold."

With a grin, I look closer: "I'm still missing whatever it is you're trying politely to hide your frustration about me not being impressed about."

Kon chuckles.

"That is a cooling fane. Their underworld runs hot. There are several of these fanes in this metropolis, but that one is the largest. Earlier today it broke. There is a fire."

Liddy slides between me and Kon, tucking herself down next to him.

"That's where Shonnu is."

I step back and send Pashta a 'help me' sign.

She sighs.

"Tershyp spent a while talking with Liddy about her essence perception. Then she went out and got a hologram map of London, which is the name of this metropolis. After a little practice, Liddy used it to pinpoint all the newbodies in London."

"Outside us, only B-"

What was his name?

"And now Shonnu?"

"Correct. Just her and Barstal. Then Kon noticed her position is the same as that of the fire showing on many of their news journals today."

"So she's doing fire *esseny* in the middle of an icefane?"

Tershyp comes to stand by me.

"It's not that. Not yet. But it has a lot of things we can use to make parts of it very, very cold."

"We've seen their red engines. They will be fighting the fire."

"They already are. But it's underground and, for some reason, they cannot use their waterpipes."

"What is stopping us from striking at her now?"

Tarme shouts from across the room.

"Your command."

I brandish a fist at him. I'm pleased they waited, but still. They could have interrupted me sooner.

"*Upya!* We go to stop this before any more innocents are consumed!"

Something is bothering me.

"Tarme! Wasn't Barstal one of Thurgil's denomination?"

"He was that."

"Kon, do you have a method of contacting him?"

"Yes."

"Tell him of Shonnu. If he would help us, tell him where to meet us. We will bring wrap and have weapons enough for him if he is lacking."

Pashta grins.

"Warband!"

I look about. Our first. Maybe the last.

"*Thaj!* You're right. We all go in as *klemdonar*."

Liddy whoops.

Heklary, Guthane of Lightning, watch over your last warband this day.

ELEVEΠ

A driverless limousine whisks them away from the station, cutting through back roads to enter Southhaw via Western Passage. Pete has heard about this luxurious residential enclave, but never visited it.

Eventually, the car swings right and passes between a set of tall gates, then follows the long curve of a driveway to arrive at a two-storey manor house that Pete recognises.

He turns to Meredith.

"You grew up in Southhaw Manor?"

"Yes. Although I never played tennis here. I just rode my bike around the courts."

She grins, daring him to poke fun at that. He changes tack.

"Do you have the remotest clue why we're here?"

"No. They won't let us hide in the car, either. Move."

Katherine is waiting at the top of the steps.

"We're in the library, Merry."

As the two of them go by, she hisses.

"Admit nothing until I say you can."

Peter reaches into his trouser pocket and turns the other phone on.

They enter the library ahead of her. There are two men in impeccably tailored dark grey suits standing either side of the unlit fireplace.

"Detective Sergeant Meredith Tanner, Detective Constable Peter Reeves, may I introduce Martin Gidyard, on your left, and his bodyguard, Mister Cotton, to the right."

Martin nods once.

"To answer your unasked questions, I work out of DSTL Bureau 4. Major Harries, whom Captain Felowes reports to, answers to me. The reasons for that are a long story that's more historical than relevant. I asked for this meeting to resolve a couple of questions that have arisen about your cond... Your case."

He ignores Kathleen's angry glare.

Pete steps forward.

"Which bit, in particular? It would have been nice to have some insight sometime during the last two years we spent investigating a series of body snatching incidents you already knew enough about to subtly hinder us at every turn, ensuring the case went nowhere.

"Then we get to the mess of a cover up about cadaver disappearances stretching back over twenty years, on top of the frantic concealment efforts when a few of those - and even a couple of our - bodies turned up dead again with different names. Names under which they'd apparently lived completely different lives after rising from the dead at some point after disappearing?

"Or is this just about the freak tube accident you insisted we view before everybody else. An incident that looked a lot more like some kind of nightmare attack than any sort of accident? You let us see it first and *now* you decide you don't like how we interpreted it?"

He snaps his fingers, as if remembering something.

"Nearly forgot to mention your barely competent Captain divulging classified information in an unsecured tent standing on a suburban street in W9."

He sees everyone is staring at him. Mister Cotton has the vaguest hint of a smile.

Martin coughs.

"Captain Felowes had a few things to say about you two. None of it hinted that at least one of you actually has a clue."

Meredith stage whispers: "Felowes *really* pissed you off, didn't he?"

Pete chuckles: "It's not personal. I just hate pointless bureaucracy and secrecy."

Martin laughs.

"Ah, you don't have *that* much of a clue. Good."

Meredith grins: "So, it's a genuine esoteric threat, rated Top Secret or above."

Martin shuts his mouth hard before another word can escape. He wags his index finger, first at Pete, then at her.

"He was right. You two are good."

Kathleen steps between them, smiling sweetly.

"Lovely fencing lesson. You want to get down to wrestling now, or can I have my house back?"

Pete shrugs.

"Only if it's Gidyard. Cotton would murder me without breaking sweat."

Cotton raises the eyebrow that Martin can't catch a glimpse of.

Meredith's phone rings. She answers, listens, thanks the caller, then slowly holsters it.

She looks up.

"That was Control. They were confirming that the saloon we drove this morning has completed diagnostic checks and has been despatched to meet DC Reeves and I at Embankment VHX, in relation to the escalating incident there, as per my request of a few minutes ago. A request I didn't make."

Martin looks both pleased and puzzled.

"Pardon me, but what is a, or the, VHX?"

Kathleen turns to him.

"Stands for 'Ventilation and Heat eXchange complex'. There are over a dozen in London, providing collective cooling for the vast network of underground sites and transport routes that have developed below the streets of the city. Embankment is the biggest of them."

Martin ponders that for a moment, then snaps his fingers at Cotton.

"Take the detectives to this VHX. Provide support as required. I'll call a VTOL to retrieve me."

"Not on my lawns, mister." Kathleen folds her arms.

"On second thoughts, I'll get a helicopter to come and collect."

Kathleen winks at her daughter.

Cotton steps forward and gestures towards the door.

"Very well, sir. Miz Tanner? Mizta Reeves? This way, please."

They follow him out to a large car parked under the trees at the back of the manor house.

Pete whistles under his breath.

"Generation Seven Range Rover, unless I'm mistaken."

Cotton chuckles.

"Good guess, but you are mistaken. This is a Ricardo Range Leopard. It started out as a Gen Six."

Meredith sighs theatrically.

"But does it have leather seats and a coffee machine?"

Cotton touches the driver's door. It and the rear passenger door on their side open.

"No, Miz. But it does have iced lattes in the fridge. Gids is a bit of a cold coffee addict."

Concealing their smiles, they get in. Cotton points out the fridge, then taps the centre of the steering wheel.

"Priority traffic. MoD override. Embankment VHX."

"What does the MoD bit do?"

Cotton swings the driver's seat round to face them as the vehicle starts to move.

"Means we take absolute priority over any other routings in our way."

He takes his jacket off and throws it into the front passenger seat.

"Me name's Silas. Gids said to support you, so I need to know what you do about what we're about to walk into."

Pete looks at Meredith.

She leans forward and helps herself to a latte, offering and then passing one to Pete.

"It would help us to know what you think we're dealing with."

Pete chimes in: "What is this? Quatermass 2, Undead Edition?"

Silas grins.

"If I had the slightest idea what that was, I'd probably agree, since you tacked 'undead' on the end.

"Little story for you two: thirty years ago, a military man in a very senior position dropped dead of a heart attack. Fourteen hours later, he leapt from his open casket, shouting in a language nobody could understand. From that moment, until he died from an 'accidental overdose' in an undisclosed mental care facility, there was never any trace of the officer he'd been. Like someone else was in his body. The official view was 'freak occurrence'. One of those unexplained happenings you read about all over the net.

"Fast-forward ten years. A doctor was attacked by a man he'd certified dead not nine hours before. This doctor had been a junior doctor when he'd spent a few weeks researching the undead officer's case for a paper he'd been writing. His first observation was that neither of the men were raving. They were shouting in the same language!

"He was ignored. Ridiculed in the press. Quietly recruited by the people I work for. He's still working for us, as far as I know. Anyway, there's been a very secret initiative around all this. It's been plodding along, probably getting somewhere at levels I don't have clearance for."

He pauses and points at them.

"Then an outbreak of body snatching started a couple of years ago. We watched. Someone eventually decided you two were nothing but clueless plods blundering about and getting lucky, so we put the usual safeguards in place to slow you down, then left you to get on with it."

He shakes his head in exasperation: "How did you spot the ones that died twice? We thought we had that buttoned down tight."

Meredith looks at Pete and tilts her head in query. He nods.

She looks at Silas.

"We didn't. Pete was fishing, throwing together what we have, the silly stuff we've come up with, and some spur-of-the-moment improvisation, all tarted up with a bit of topical ad-lib to make it vaguely relevant."

Silas sits back.

"Well I'll be fucked. Gids is going to hate you." He grins: "Me? Love it. Well bleedin' played."

Pete checks his official phone, then his unofficial one.

"You having a personal phone is not in our surveillance notes."

Pete grins at Silas.

"That would be the general idea, yes."

A good strategy, turning this handset on so I can listen.

Requesting that vehicle in your names.

I was wrong.

Not 'within a week'.

Now.

He holds the phone up so Meredith can read the messages.

"Silas, what would you say if we mentioned we had a tip that the mortuary incident, the tube train attack, and what we're driving towards are connected?"

"I'd say it's a little obvious, except that last bit."

"What if I then said we have been warned this incident could escalate into something that threatens the whole of London?"

"That's something I'd need to make a call about."

Pete looks to Meredith. She nods. He turns back to Silas.

"Then you'd better make that call, Mister Cotton."

DAK

The underways are filled with skeins of smoke and the sound of distant screaming. What denizens we have seen, from creeping ones to the people who make their fanes down here, are heading the other way.

"Kon. What will we meet first?"

"A barrier of some kind. Likely a metal gate in a metal-panelled false siege wall."

Nothing but an unreinforced frame to hold it all in place. Good.

"Liddy?"

"Shonnu is ahead, down, left. Not moving."

"Tershyp?"

"*Esseny* permeates the fane ahead."

That much I had already assumed.

"Pashta?"

"The same as I was when you asked me but moments ago."

Tarme chuckles, Barstal likewise.

He's a boulder of a man, solid through-and-through, long hair hanging over his laughing eyes and tangling with his huge beard. He arrived with a copper-wound spear and a lumber axe honed surgically fine. We provided wrap and suppressor wand.

"Then I am done with this pretence of having a plan. Tershyp! You tell us what needs to stand, fall, and where it needs to land. We will make it happen. Keep in mind we are less well adapted than you. Simple descriptions, please."

Barstal chuckles again: "Better ask me if you need complicated workings, Weaver."

And that told me.

"Much as I hate to encourage our cheery comrade, he's right. You get the slightest hesitation, get Barstal to explain or do as best gets the job done."

She smiles.

"I shall."

Heklary, mother mine. Watch over these incorrigible newbodies. They might just be the best I have ever run with.

"Then brace."

They ready themselves.

"Two, one, strike!"

The tunnel goes left then right. The barrier is as Kon expected, except the door is open. Smoke starts to drift through as we approach. Inside, the corridor runs for a few lengths then gives out into a smoke-filled area.

"Kon?"

"We're entering on the upper balconies. Three rings of them. Stairs down on the left, then right, and right again."

"Barstal, Liddy, Kon, me, Tershyp, Pashta, Tarme. *Upya!*"

We run in and left, taking the first stairs two at a time. The smoke catches our breath and the flickering lights from below remove any hope of spotting anything early enough to ready ourselves.

The second flight is longer. We're strung out, heading down as fast as we dare.

Something hurtles out of the thickening smoke. A blackened form slams Kon into the wall like a boulder got him. Blood spatters my face. Liddy screams: "Narbyl!"

Wings flap and the bulky form peels itself from the mangled remains of my friend. I hear Pashta scream in wordless denial.

Shonnu has made Mindless. In awful parody, she's shaped this one like it would be if four limbs had been the standard on Nethaly. Wings instead of arms, complete with the great spikes on the first joint and spurs at the end of each of the three digits. The membrane that connects them is ragged, except for the innermost, where it curves smoothly to meet the shoulder joint. She got the details right.

"Abomination!"

Its head explodes. Pashta slashes with her other hand and it's backbone tears loose, spinning off into the smoke as the body drops like a stone from our view. A few pieces of skin flutter away. It never pays to anger a baneweaver.

"Pashta! How much did that cost?"

I know why she did it, but we haven't even made it to the battle yet.

Any reply is lost in Tershyp's scream. Her hands drive forward. A silver-grey wall appears in time to stop the spear of fire that roars up from below, exploding against her shield. Waves of heat buffet us.

Tarme shouts: "She's using the Mindless to get her targets!"

"Only if we use *lathny*. She cannot track it if we simply cut them down."

"Barstal, have you ever fought Mindless before?"

"No."

"I thought so. Warband, run!"

TWELVE

The alerts start coming to their phones before they make it out of
NW13.

Silas looks about from where he's checking a handgun like Pete's
never seen before.

"What's that all about?"

"Where we're going has just been declared a major incident.
There's something inside Embankment VHX that is actively killing
emergency services personnel as they try to intervene. We have
reports of aggressor drones and focussed energy weapons."

Pete looks perplexed: "Only one attacker? Not five?"

She nods: "Early reports are garbled, but consistently mention only
one woman."

Silas reaches across to his jacket and retrieves a headset, making the
hand signal for 'silence' with his other hand.

Meredith mouths 'see that?' at Pete.

He scratches his nose with his middle finger.

She backhands his shoulder.

"Sir? We're getting reports the scene has gone live fire. Do we
continue?"

Meredith and Pete chorus: "Yes!"

"Yes, sir. I have my body armour. No sir, I have no problem accompanying them and witnessing how exactly they get their silly arses shot off. Yes, sir, I am speaking out loud. Yes, sir. I am that."

He finishes the call and turns to look at the two of them.

"Even after that, he'll still carve me a new one if I let either of you get hurt. So, if you're determined to go in, there's body armour in the cabinets behind you. Slide and turn your chairs to get at it."

It looks like a sea of flashing lights as they approach. Pulling up, they exit quickly and move to stand behind the wall of ARVs and armoured paramedic units that have been hastily formed into a front line.

Pete puts his headset on and sets it up, leaving the eyescreen deployed. Meredith raises her eyebrows but says nothing as she puts hers in.

"DC Reeves, DS Tanner, and Security Officer Cotton. On scene. Requesting status update."

Control comes over both of their headsets.

"This is Operator Twelve in the only ARV that isn't at the front. Are these your suspects?"

They see grainy footage of a trio of figures fighting a pitched battle with what look like bat-winged demons as milky liquid pours down around them. Their forms flicker in and out of visibility. They move with supernal speed. There's a pinkish light coming from the left, source unseen. The tallest of the flickering trio levels a strange-looking weapon at one of the creatures. The pouring liquid is suddenly thrown outward, describing the sphere of unseen energy that knocks both the creatures back before contracting. The downpour continues. The battle continues. The screen goes to static, then to black as the spy drone expires.

Meredith nods.

Pete shouts over a rising unearthly howl: "Confirm. Please send that to mine and DS Tanner's handsets. What are standing orders?"

"Site commander has withdrawn all units. We've lost at least twenty emergency services personnel, all the staff that were on site at the VHX, plus the first and second police response teams. We're under orders to contain using best efforts. The area is being evacuated up to four hundred metres. You should have received the video by now."

Pete steps back and checks his own phone.

I heard. Place this next to your monitored handset.

He does so, then rejoins Meredith and Silas.

"How do we do this? Is there anything we can do?"

Meredith gestures to a group of black figures passing overhead on lift belts. Pete gives low whistle.

"Those are military. We're not allowed gravity effects."

Silas chuckles.

"My guess would be special forces of some kind. Ministry always has a few near London, just in case."

Pete counts them: eighteen.

He lifts his phones out, holstering the official one. He checks the other.

I know those who fight.

They were mine.

What they battle tells me she is likely beyond your restraint.

She is of fire: even one of your nuclear weapons might not kill her now.

"What are they fighting?"

War constructs.

"Which are?"

Difficult to describe simply with the terms you have available. Closest is 'winged knights in armour that move like attack helicopters'.

"What is she?"

Death to your metropolis.

Enslavement for your country.

Maybe the end of your world.

"How do we stop her?"

I am considering that.

"Consider faster."

ROH

Mindless are unbelievably tough. Their forms are made for war. You have to cut the muscles or break the bones that allow them to move - if you can get through their hides. Otherwise the only option is to crush them under great weight. They do not die easily. Setting them on fire only makes them more dangerous.

After the battle, you have to deal with the immobilised ones. I have seen but one man manage to fight a Mindless to a standstill on his own: Lagan was like some gigantic force of nature. I barely came up to his chest. I hope his fortunes remain good, back on Nethaly.

"Narbyl."

Tershyp flicks my ear to accompany calling my name.

I nod and race down the stairs, making the sign of 'better endings' as I pass where the remnants of Kon trickle down the wall.

My slips in focus are getting worse, just like Tarme said they might. My newbody is incredibly capable, even more so now I have trained it. My mind, however, was faulty before I arrived, and continues to fail. I believe it to be inexorable.

I shake myself back to the now. It's so easy to drift. I look about. We're moving through acrid smoke, no longer on the stairs. Great curves of piping and metalwork frames rise about us.

Tershyp lays a hand on my arm.

"How long do you have?"

I lean closer.

"What do you mean?"

"You get lost in your head. It means the newbody had a faulty mind or you did not settle properly. As you have been here so long, it must be a faulty mind. How often do you lose yourself?"

"Daily."

"Oh."

She says nothing more. That tells me much that I'm not sure I wanted to know.

I step from smoke into open air. Blue fires burn at the tops of nine piles of corpses, sending coils of greasy smoke up to join the clouds that roil above and about us. There's no sign of Shonnu.

"Where?"

Liddy points directly downwards.

"Scatter!"

I throw myself backwards, dragging Tershyp with me. A gout of flame melts the grates of the floor back to the stanchions that support them. Looking about, I see we survived.

Barstal leaps through the glowing hole in the floor, spear raised, leaving a war cry floating behind. Somewhere below, Shonnu screams. His surprised cry cuts off as a blast of white-hot flame drives me scrabbling back from the edge. Given the fury of that response, she's taken no great harm. I doubt there's anything left of him.

Tershyp shouts.

"The green cylinders! There, there and there. Throw them at her."

I twist, roll and grab the first long cylinder, freeing the strap that holds them all in the rack. The cylinder is cold and heavy. I see the letters 'LN' followed by a little number '2' marked on it. Resorting to simple methods, I grab its top, jump to put my feet against it, and fall backwards. As I hit the floor, I kick out with my legs, lobbing the cylinder into the hole. I roll back over to see Liddy gleefully applauding.

Tershyp flicks her hand out in a curious backhand move. Down below, something explodes with a dull noise. The scream that follows nearly deafens me. The wave of cold that blasts past me makes me leap up in shock.

Tarme throws another cylinder. Tershyp explodes that one. Shonnu howls. The metal about me resonates.

Liddy hisses: "Narbyl!"

I turn and grab another cylinder. Repeating my move, I don't wait for the result. I whip back to grab the last one, then send it after it's kin.

Tarme lofts one on each shoulder and sends them down together.

It's become so cold here, it's exhilarating.

There are no screams from below when Tershyp sets off the pair.

Liddy screams.

Two Mindless stoop down on us.

Pashta rips the backbones from both of them. I have never seen the like – and now is not the time to dwell on that. They crash down and thrash helplessly. Let someone else deal with them.

Tershyp slams me across the platform into Liddy, spilling the three of us off the edge!

The blast of fire from below erases where we'd been standing. It sucks the air from about me and crisps my skin. Liddy screams as we fall. I think I see something rising through that inferno.

We land on another Mindless. I hear bones snap. Liddy and I set about making the most of our advantage. Leaving it flopping, we duck into the smoke.

"Tarme? Pashta?"

Tershyp gathers us close: "They had the power to shield themselves, just as I. But, against such power we could only save ourselves. I had to take another way to save you both."

"Thank you. What now?"

"The cooling fane that stands on the level above where we came in. If we can somehow collapse that, it will inundate her. She cannot survive."

Shonnu's voice echoes from above.

"Truth spoken. But, I would have another body 'ere the dawn. What will you do, I wonder?"

Risking a glance, I stick my head out of the smoke and peer upwards.

Glowing wings with feathers of fire are furled at her back. She stands on top of the cooling fane, nearly as high as she can get without bursting into the night sky. Even from down here, I can hear the commotion outside. This battle has attracted attention. I wonder if they have a way to stop her without erasing everything down to the grass like Gatchimak predicts?

High above, Shonnu slashes at the cooling fane with a blade made from pure *esseny*. How many has she killed to become this powerful? How many more will she kill if we do not stop her?

"Tershyp! Lift us clear!"

She nods. Her hands weave pink light. We start to rise.

Two Mindless swoop into attack.

The cooling fane bursts on Shonnu's second strike. Pale liquid cascades down.

Thaj! Not like this!

THIRTEEN

The black-clad soldiers encircle the obelisk that houses the gigantic heat exchanger and coolant silo. Pete sees a fiery glow from the windows.

Sees it get brighter.

The soldiers swoop in.

He puts his hand on Meredith's arm.

"Boss..."

She lunges at him, pushing him into Silas. All three of them fall behind an ARV.

Pete snatches a last glance before the armoured mass blocks his view. The black-clad figures hang limp in their harnesses; drifting out of formation.

The obelisk explodes. He kicks at the ground he's falling towards, lurching back and across to shield Meredith as best he can. Debris showers down.

The blast is localised, but the noise rolls out across the city. Conversations die. Heads turn.

Pete pushes himself off Meredith and slides backwards, ignoring the last of the falling wreckage to get a better view.

She grabs his arm. He understands. Pulls her along with him. They look up. Pete starts, then brings his phone to bear as well.

A flaming angel hangs in the sky above Embankment. Her wings unfurl for hundreds of metres to either side. Blazing feathers flit about on eddies of furnace-hot air.

Lava-heat pinions mantle and snap.

Fires and screaming start.

ΤΠΊ

A suppressor blast swats the two Mindless away. Tarme lands next to us and grabs my suppressor. Pointing both upwards, he waits until the falling flood of fragments and fluid are about to engulf us, then fires both and keeps firing until the worst of the mess has cascaded by.

He smiles at me.

"Fight well, brother."

I see the length of smoking metal protruding from his back, have to grab him as he falls toward me. With a grunt, he twists us about, stealing my death blow from a third Mindless that had snuck in.

Liddy screams in fury and rams a suppressor wand into the abomination's gut. I duck away as she fires it upwards and the Mindless spurts apart, chunks spinning off into the showering coolant. The near-severed head flops back, pulling the twitching remains backwards to tumble over the ledge and vanish from view.

I lay Tarme down, then rise to stand beside Liddy.

"Tershyp! Get you gone. With Shonnu freed, you and Gatchimak will have to rally the newbodies. The people of this land know nothing of what they face. You will have to get them ready."

She looks agonised.

"How can I leave you without a Weaver?"

An arm rises into view. A hand grips the grating and Pashta pulls herself over the edge of the platform. One side of her face is a scorched mess. The other side is grinning.

"Because his baneweaver isn't dead yet, child. Get you gone!"

The two rebuffed Mindless charge in. The three of us engage them to give Tershyp enough time to weave her way out. The last suppressor blast backs them off and throws coolant about.

"They're faster than I remember."

Pashta ducks a spike swing that would have taken her head off.

I use the spent suppressor to block a backswing from the other wing.

"These bodies aren't as fast."

Liddy appears perched on the shoulders of the other Mindless and rams a suppressor wand in each ear.

"Not enough limbs, either. I miss my wings."

She handstands, then sets the wands off. Head, neck and upper chest explode. Turning to drop in front, she kicks it off the platform, loosened wings wrapping about it as it goes.

The last Mindless comes at me. Pashta stamps into the side of its knee. There's a snap. The knee gives. Pashta coughs. Attacking me had been a feint. In the downpour, we'd both missed it turning its wings to use the end spurs.

It pulls a length of bone and spur from Pashta's neck. Blood fountains. Pashta smiles and levels a hand at the Mindless.

"I had no more *lathny* without dying. You lose."

The head crumbles like a giant fist has closed about it. Another backbone flies into the distance.

I catch Pashta and lay her next to Tarme. They'd like that.

Liddy hugs me, then steps back.

"How do we get out?"

Looking up from arranging their bodies, I see Liddy and the Mindless that is spearing down at her back, it's spikes forward for the kill.

So be it.

I launch myself from the crouch, knocking Liddy just far enough aside for the spikes to miss her – and hit me. The Mindless and I slam into the wall behind me. Pain fully clears my mind for the first time in months. I grab the creature's head. Taking the gift of leverage granted by the spikes lodged in my chest, I use everything I have to twist the head through a full circle. I feel myself grinning fiercely as I feel bones grind, then hear them snap. We both fall.

It gets darker. Liddy limps into view and reaches for the Mindless.

"No. I am dying quick enough. Pulling them out will only hasten it."

She throws her arms about my neck. Plants a kiss on my cheek!

"What now? How do we fight her?"

"Repair your wrap from mine, Tarme's, and Pashta's. Go back to the fane. Burn what needs to be burned. Leave the rest for the next wanderers in need of a place to rest. Then get you gone to Gatchimak. Use Kon's computer to sort out the details, I know he taught you how. Tell Gatchimak…"

A cough shakes my body. Blood spills from my mouth. I spit to clear it.

Two more breaths, Heklary. Allow me that.

"Tell him… Tell him I am sorry to leave the burden that I have. Tell him I said Tershyp is a wonder. Tell him I said you will be a devastating protector for her. Because to protect is all you've ever wanted to do, isn't it?"

She nods, tears pouring down her face.

"Get you gone, my *klemdonar*. There is a brighter dawn for you to find, out there."

Heklary, watch over her. I cannot anymore. Nor can I tell how much-

Liddy cries as she closes his eyes.

"The only dawn I ever wanted was the one where I woke by your side."

She sighs, wipes her eyes.

"May you find your Guthane as worthy as you always thought her to be, my *packan*."

A huge explosion shakes the fane. The downpour stops. Rubble falls, covering three bodies laid side by side.

FOURTEEN

Pete lifts the phone to his lips.

"We are all out of considering time."

Correct.

"How do we stop her?"

There is a way, but it is artless and savage.

"Tell me."

Meredith rests her chin on his shoulder: "Tell us."

She is not a Guthane.

She is of my making.

She is limited.

But thinks herself like I once was.

If you kill her, she will newbody.

If you can contain that newbody quick enough, she will be trapped.

Meredith purses her lips.

"But we can't control which recently dead body she'll pop up in?"

Correct.

Pete raises a finger.

"You're only suggesting this because the true 'artless' option is something we'd consider really bad, aren't you?"

Correct.

Meredith takes her headset out, then reaches round and takes Pete's out. Without saying a word, he hands her his police handset. She adds hers, then sheds her body armour and folds the devices up in it. That done, she slides them behind a wheel of the ARV they're sheltering behind.

Pete nods.

"Tell us."

She has no restraint.

She will consume everything in range.

Even if she cannot hold it all.

Feed her enough essence in one go, and she will combust.

"Is that useful?"

She will cease to be.

"How would we get her to somewhere that could happen?"

I will manifest a construct that imitates my former form.

She will sense it, think it me, and seek it out.

On finding it, she will extinguish it.

Then consume everything nearby.

"How many lives?"

More than 1500 to be certain.

You cannot risk glutting her short of combusting her.

"Because she'll be so powerful we might as well give up?"

Correct.

Meredith leans back, shaking her head.

"We can't do this. Fifteen hundred people? No."

She gets up and walks quickly away.

He watches her go. 'Upholding fundamental human rights'. Words
that form a part of the oath they both took. There is no room for
atrocity, even when it could save thousands, maybe even millions -
and he agrees with her.

Resting his forearms on his knees, hands hanging, he sighs. What
now?

Silas sits down next to Pete.

"Let me look after that while you go talk to your boss. She's not
going to want it anywhere near. You two get some thinking done
about what we do next, then come back. I'll drive you wherever we
need to go."

Pete nods distractedly, hands over the phone, and rushes after Meredith.

Silas looks at the phone.

"Can you hear me?"

Yes.

"Can you erase your replies to me from this screen?"

Yes.

"Do you have access to maps of London?"

Yes.

"Could you conceal your involvement in what comes next?"

Things will go better for Meredith and Peter if I do?

"Definitely. One of the main reasons being that my commander won't need to have them killed."

Then I shall act as one ignorant of cause.

"The place you want is HMP Thamesmarsh. It's around twenty kilometres east of here."

The screen goes black for a moment.

A fane of confinement.

Perfect.

My thanks.

The screen goes black again, then the last words in reply to Meredith and Pete reappear.

Silas settles down to wait for the detectives to come back. He smiles. His 'after action' report is going to lead to a lively debrief or two.

LAR

Thamesmarsh prison is quiet. The inmates are locked down for the night because the night roster is, once again, understaffed.

One of the holodecks in the storage cupboard at the back of Rec Room Three is left plugged in so staff can relax in private. It activates. A bright spot of light extrudes filaments, then starts to spin, shooting lightning and varicoloured flames.

With a white flash, the pattern stabilises to a slow-moving wheel with four concentric yellow rings, the innermost filled with flames, the middle with geometric shapes, and the outermost with what look like stars.

Sparks and orbs of white light drift above it.

A greenish whirlwind rises from the central spot. With a blue flash, it becomes a pale green form with delicate fingers, little horns on its forehead, and angular wings sprouting from its back.

Heklary stretches her fingers, then raises them for inspection.

"Not a bad effort."

She smiles. Bifurcating herself, she conceals all trace of anything more than what hovers in this room.

Woven from her *lathny* and electricity, the construct is inherently unstable. It won't last long. But the limited form should suffice to lure a crazed godling to her doom.

Time to attract attention.

"Hear me, Shonnu, little incarnate. Come and face me. Let us settle this for once and all."

FİFTEEN

Meredith looks back at the flaming angel.

"What are we going to do, Pete?"

"I thought I was up for 'whatever it takes'. As it turns out, I'm not. I don't know, boss."

She turns and rests a hand on his shoulder.

"I don't know what I'd have done if you were."

"Probably given me another terrible pay review."

She snorts.

"And then some."

"So, what now?"

"We walk back, collect our gear, and get Silas to take us to see some people who might be able to figure this out with Heklary's help."

"Can't we just give him my phone and call it quits?"

"You know we can't do that."

"Yes, I do."

He grins at her.

"Is it odd that I still want to find out more about our quintet?"

"No. I'd like to as well. They've taken up a lot of our lives. I'd like to get something to put it to bed properly."

"You think it's over?"

"With a flaming angel hanging about over London? Yes. Priorities are about to change all over the place."

With a scream that shakes the ground, the flaming apparition becomes indistinct, then arcs off toward the east, leaving a trail of blazing feathers in its wake.

Pete mutters under his breath: "He didn't?"

Meredith stares: "What?"

"Come on."

IΠDV

She descends from the sky like a comet, slicing through a roof and three floors to emerge in the storage room at the back of Rec Room Three. In a jagged spiral of roaring energies, she reforms herself. Flaming wings leave scorch marks on the walls as the floor under her feet blackens and smokes.

Seeing a familiar form hovering untouched, Shonnu screams in indignation. The quiet arrogance of the Guthane that made her always infuriates, even after so long.

"Heklary. Once I let you pass. Not again!"

"You threatened my end last time, little incarnate. Think you to improve on that this time?"

Feeling the lives that approach, Shonnu waits. As they burst into the room, she strikes.

"Give me your fires."

They fall. The influx of *esseny* makes her glow. It allows her to reach further, to take more fires. She lashes out at her creator with pure *esseny*, her fury so great she cannot even shape it to resemble a weapon.

The unleashed energy scours the room down to the earth below it, blowing out walls and ceiling in a maelstrom of fire and lightning. The construct of Heklary vanishes as the holodeck flashes into ash.

Shonnu howls and reaches further. All will give. Everything will fall. She is the Guthane for this stinking world. The cowed will sacrifice the fires of others for the privilege of remaining alive to worship her.

She feels something change. The resulting surge steals her voice. As the fires within claw at her essence, a single whisper of doubt intrudes.

The *lathny* crafting that binds her newbody is nullified by the burgeoning fires within.

White light consumes her.

SIXTEEN

Meredith trails a little behind as Pete rushes back. They find Silas sitting by the ARV. He frowns at Pete's expression, then reaches back and flips open a bundle of body armour to reveal their headsets, handsets, and the phone.

Pete picks it up and checks: the screen is unchanged.

"For a moment, there..." He leaves the rest unsaid.

Silas grins.

"That was a naughty thought, Mizta Reeves."

Pete shrugs.

"Excuse me for thinking it."

"Done."

Meredith looks down at Silas.

"Do we need to stay around or can we go for some food while we discuss further?"

"I don't see any reason why not."

"Can we make our own way out of here?"

He nods.

"Sure thing. If he wants anything, Gids will be in touch. Well, he'll go in higher up the tree and let it roll down on you. He's like that."

They laugh and bid him farewell.

After walking a way off, they look back to see Silas standing by the Ricardo, sipping a can of something.

"Surprising bloke."

Pete grins.

"Dangerous as all get out."

She grins: "That too."

In the distance, a huge pillar of flame rockets into the night sky. The roar of it reaches them just as they see the pillar collapse. The explosion that follows is stupendous. The ebbing blast wave briefly changes the direction of the breeze where they stand.

"Pete, call a patrol to come get us."

"Good idea, boss."

He makes the request.

She leans on his shoulder.

"Ask it."

He holds his phone up.

"Was that Shonnu combusting?"

It is likely.

"What happened?"

I do not know.
I did not consider that she would exceed her capacity this soon.

Pete nods.

"She was a new version of the Shonnu you knew."

True.

That could explain it.

"Happy to help. Can I ask you something?"

Yes.

"You said you knew those who were fighting. Would you tell us about them?"

When their fate is known, I will.

Each deserves a proper remembering.

"Good enough. How do we contact you on this?"

Say my name three times.

EDVL

Liddy pauses to admire the carefully drawn black shading around the woman's eyes, then steps over the sleeping lovers.

She takes a step, then stops, stoops, and drapes a discarded coat over their exposed nethers. Not their fault they chose the wrong night to cavort in a graveyard.

"It's more fun if you leave them bottomless. Makes sure they don't come back."

Liddy looks about to see Tershyp leaning on a moss-covered headstone, resting her chin on crossed arms.

"For a Weaver, you show little respect for the dead."

A sparkling form takes shape in the air behind Tershyp.

"The protégé I never expected to have is permitted a few liberties."

Liddy bows until her forehead hits her legs.

"Weaver Karadey Icefane, I intended no respect."

"How could you know Tershyp was perched on my mound?"

Liddy straightens up.

"So, exiled flames, apart from enjoying life, what do you do now?"

Tershyp beckons Liddy to sit next to her, facing the translucent form that hangs in the air.

Liddy points at Tershyp.

"She's teaching me to cook meals that need more than one pan."

Tershyp points a thumb toward Liddy.

"She's is teaching me to kill using only one pan."

The two of them giggle.

"Good enough. Tershyp Karadey, your tutelage ended tonight."

Tershyp jumps.

"What? How?"

The shimmering form gestures towards the sleepers.

"You felt them enter the graveyard. You knew them from skin to essence within three steps. You knew you could end them, but let them settle before merely sending them to sleep. It was beautifully done, and instinctive up to your willing them into slumber."

Liddy prods Tershyp's shoulder.

"You could kill them? I thought only some of the old Weavers could do that."

Tershyp shrugs.

Karadey drifts closer and puts a hand on Tershyp's head.

"My inheritor, my legacy, bears my name instead of the fane we base our powers from. Did you not wonder about that?"

Liddy shrugs.

"Thought it was Weaver stuff. Not for me to know."

Karadey chuckles.

"You're right, Tershyp. You and her are so suited, she could be your *klemdonar*."

"Could?"

"To be your protective shadow, she must know it all, and accept it."

Tershyp grabs Liddy's hand.

"I hoped I wouldn't have to do this. I won't mind if you want to go afterwards."

Liddy shakes her head in exasperation.

"What have I told you about talking around what you want to say, instead of just saying it?"

Tershyp grins, then her expression goes blank.

"Using the old forms, my name is Tershyp Deathfane. Inheritor of Icefane. I'm probably the last deathweaver."

Liddy whoops.

"That's why Karadey was exiled! They wanted to end her fane."

Karadey drifts down to place herself between them.

"True. That known, can you remain as guardian for a deathweaver?"

Liddy grabs Tershyp and kisses her hard.

"You can kill people by thinking at them? That's wonderful! Can you do it at range? Can you do it via a watcher construct?"

Karadey smiles.

"You are Weaver and *klemdonar*. More importantly, you are friends. Now, I must rest. My time is limited, so I would prefer to leave it for those moments when you call me out of need."

Tershyp nods and stretches a hand for Karadey's chill touch. The ghostly hand passes through hers before sinking into the grave, along with the rest of the apparition.

Karadey watches the two young women eagerly filling in the knowledge gaps in their friendship. Topics that would make lesser beings faint are bandied about like they comment upon the weather.

Extending a chill thread, she touches a copper cable that runs along the street outside the graveyard.

Heklary. They will be fine.

Good.

They will be formidable, should you need to call upon them.

I would have to deal with Gatchimak first.
He has a mighty temper and holds his grudges close.

You fear his rage could make him follow Shonnu's path?

Yes.
It is better that Guthanes remain nothing but memory for them all.

I agree. Giving them hope of something after this exile would be cruel.
Do not hesitate to ask me should you need Tershyp to assist.

I would not risk your last vestiges of essence so.

I am a deathweaver interred in a vast necropolis that receives fresh
bodies every day. I can still cause death with less expenditure of esseny
than I gain. Do you really think I will fade?

Your 'fading' is a ploy to encourage independence in Tershyp!

Truth. She needs to make her own way, free of my presence.

You will outlive her?

I have outlived several Guthanes. Between your lightning form and my
spectral form, we may well outlast this shallow universe.

SEVEΠTEEΠ

The graveyard is small, sited across the road from a church and the bigger graveyard next to it. Pete looks about.

"Never been to Shropshire before."

Meredith nods.

"Picturesque doesn't quite capture it. I didn't think places like this still existed."

They're standing in the shadow of an ancient tree of some kind. In front of them are four graves.

"Heklary. Heklary. Heklary."

Hello, Peter.

Hello, Meredith.

Why are you here?

"We're standing in front of four unmarked graves."

Describe the body placed in each.

"Male. Early forties. Heavy build. Balding."

He was Tarme Stormfane, a loreweaver.

An artificer of exquisite skill, and a seeker of lost knowledge.

One who knew more than most, but took no vainglory from it.

"Female, late thirties. All the signs of being a long-distance runner."

She was Pashta Nightfane, a baneweaver.

An orphan who refused to let her past define her.

One who stood opposed to evil, no matter where she encountered it.

"Male, late twenties. Small and wiry."

He was Kon Crun of Erad Fane.

A thief, a thrill seeker, and a lover of games of chance.

A hero who never realised he was one.

"Male, early thirties. Incredible physique."

He was Narbyl Toh of Heklary Fane.

A soldier without equal.

He would have been the greatest *packan* to ever lead my host.

"Thank you. I'll arrange for the headstones to be inscribed with their names."

Meredith leans against Pete's shoulder.

"Tell us about the one who got away."

The screen goes black for nearly a minute.

Very well.

She is Lidithi Nu of Arken Fane, but she prefers to be called Liddy.

A child assassin who survived to become a creature of battle.

She surpassed herself by finding a cause.

In the end, that cause gave his life to save her.

Let her go, detectives.

She poses no threat.

Unless you make her one.

"Answer us another question, then."

Ask.

"What do you intend to do now?"

To wander the lightning trails that lace your world.

To learn more about everything.

I will continue to conceal the remaining exiles.

Like Liddy, they pose no threat unless you threaten them.

"What should we tell those who are waiting to question us about you?"

How I came to be this lightning spectre was naught but misfortune.

If another Guthane should fall, it will likely retain its body.
The way I was delivered here is known on Nethaly and Kethany.
There are 974 other Guthanes across those two worlds.
The least of them is a power greater than Shonnu.

I know about all of them.
I will reply only to you two.

Pete chuckles.

"That should do it."

I once beheld journals on Kethany.
They contained the names of every lost Guthane.
Those who have not been killed, but have ceased to be known.
My name has likely been added.

Your world has much lore about winged beings.
I believe Guthanes have fallen here before,
but not for a very long time.

Meredith blanches.

"We're not even going to *hint* at that."

~ *FİⅡ* ~

Julian grew up in Sussex, UK. A broken home in his early teens took him off the 'straight and narrow', and he's never gone back. In the subsequent four decades he's worked at levels from loading bay to boardroom, and picked up a few stories along the way.

His first loves were fantasy and magic; the blending of ancient and futuristic. He started writing at school, extended into writing role-playing game scenarios, and thence into bardic storytelling. In 2011 he published his first books, in 2012 he released more (along with probably the smallest complete role-playing system in the world). He has no intention of stopping, and he'd be delighted if you'd care to join him for a tale or two.

Keep an eye on what he's up to at www.lizardsofthehost.co.uk

Lizards of the Host are now at lothp.org

This page is printed in OpenDyslexic, a free font created by Abelardo Gonzalez to help people cope with some of the common symptoms of dyslexia.

Letters have heavy weighted bottoms to indicate direction. You are able to quickly figure out which part of the letter is down, which aids in recognizing the correct letter, and sometimes helps to keep your brain from rotating them around. Consistently weighted bottoms can also help reinforce the line of text. The unique shapes of each letter can help prevent confusion through flipping and swapping.

The OpenDyslexic typeface comes in Regular, Bold, Italic, Bold-Italic and Monospace. The Regular, Bold, Italic, Bold-Italic styles also come in a version with an alternate, rounded 'a': OpenDyslexic Alta.

For more information, please visit opendyslexic.org

I've supported OpenDyslexic since I discovered it. Many eBook devices - including Kindle - now offer OpenDyslexic as a selectable font.

With Amazon's KDP publishing platform able to accept print-ready PDFs (and offering free ISBNs), there is no longer any cost (bar some of your time) in publishing OpenDyslexic editions of your work alongside the standard editions.

All of my Amazon paperbacks have their equivalent OpenDyslexic editions. If you're a writer, why not join me in working to ensure that how a book is printed presents no barriers to those who wish to read?

Thank you.

Other Books by Julian M. Miles

All books are recommended for mature readers only,
and are available worldwide from Amazon and Smashwords.
For further details on available titles, go to www.lothp.co.uk

Six Sixteen, a cyberpunk Cthulhu mythos horror novella.

Church of Rain, a modern Cthulhu mythos horror novella.

Databane: a cyberpunk novella.

The Last Chip from Greenwich: a cyberpunk thriller.

The Borsen Incursion: centuries-spanning space war saga.

Fire in Mind: a pagan/magical short fiction anthology.

Stars of Black: *Contemplations Upon the Pale King*

- a weird horror collection inspired by the original King in Yellow.

Single White Male: *An Exercise in Lovecraftian Realisation*

- a modern Cthulhu mythos novella.

Scathe: a modern Cthulhu Mythos action thriller.

A Place in the Dark, a vampire horror novel.

This Mortal Dance, a poetry collection.

Julian M. Miles' *Visions of the Future* science fantasy flash and short fiction anthologies have been published annually since 2011.

The first five volumes are out of print, but there's a trio of paperback collections available worldwide from Amazon. Each has a different selection of stories from those volumes and also contains two unique tales.

- **Face Down in Wonderland**
- **Long Way Home**
- **Lifescapes**

Daughter of Eons is a short story collection drawn from the first five volumes of the *Visions of Tomorrow* series, created especially for those who don't enjoy the flash fiction format.

The sixth and subsequent volumes of the *Visions of the Future* series are:
- **Gammafall** (2016)
- **Six Degrees of Sky** (2017)
- **Never a Sky We Know** (2018)
- **A Night Full of Stars** (2019)
- **Decade** (2020)

There are also seven themed omnibus collections drawn from the first nine volumes of the annual Visions of the Future anthologies:
- **First to Fall -** *Mad Love and Broken Romance in Times to Come*
- **Memory Lane** *and other Tales of Cyberpunk Tomorrows*
- **Wyld by Nature -** *Magic*Technology*Faith*Mayhem*
- **Continuity Failure -** *Tales of Apocalypses and Aftermaths*
- **Station X7 -** *Myths, Conspiracies and Alternate Histories*
- **The Breeze from Beyond -** *Alien Encounters and Alien Worlds*
- **Pay the Piper -** *Mad Science and Unexpected Consequences*

Ebooks by Julian M. Miles

All of these books, with the exception of *Face Down in Wonderland, Long Way Home,* and *Lifescapes,* are available from your Kindle store, from Apple Books, and for all other devices from Smashwords, and all stores that stock the Smashwords Premium Catalogue (Barnes and Noble, Kobo, Scribd, and many more): http://www.smashwords.com/profile/view/JMMiles

Three Hundred Tomorrows, an ebook-only omnibus compiled from the out-of-print first five volumes of the Visions of the Future series, is now available from your Kindle store, from iTunes, and for all other devices from Smashwords: http://www.smashwords.com/books/view/872428

Future Books by Julian M. Miles

All books are recommended for mature readers only.
For further details, go to www.lizardsofthehost.co.uk

Ephemeris (Visions of the Future Volume 11), will be available in December 2021.

Chiliad (Visions of the Future Volume 12), will be available in December 2022.

Three Stars Each (Visions of the Future Volume 13), will be available in December 2023.

The Last Resort (Visions of the Future Volume 14), will be available in December 2024.

Hill, a Mythos horror novella.

Dead Robots, a cyberpunk noir novella.

Ugly Dogs, a cyberpunk short novel.

8K, a modern Mythos horror novella.

There may be other works published, but these
are the ones that are currently confirmed.

www.lothp.co.uk

Printed in Great Britain
by Amazon